BOOKS MAKE
BRAINZ
TASTE BAD

~~ELI CRANOR~~ *Dash Storey!*

Illustrated by
DANIEL FREEMAN

BARE B☠NES BOOKS

Bare Bones Books - United States

ISBN 978-1-7353221-0-0

First Edition

For Mom... duh!

WARNING!

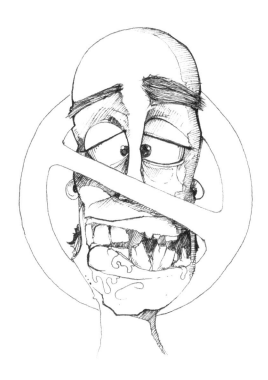

THIS BOOK COULD SAVE your life. I'm serious, *dead* serious.

My name is Dashiell Storey, but everybody calls me *Dash*. Sweet name, right? And what's even cooler, I'm writing this story.

And this isn't just any story. It's a *book*. A book that

could—if you read every page, carefully, if you pay really close attention—save your life!

Don't forget that last part. It's super important.

And don't forget this either: *Books make brainz taste bad.* Brainz with a "Z" because that's how zombies say it.

Zombies are out there. You probably even know some but just don't realize it yet. I'm serious. I'm going to tell you about the most epic week of my twelve-year-old life. I'm not going to leave anything out. I can't. It's all too important. I won't make anything up, either.

I won't tell you how I went all video game zombie slayer on the domes of the undead. I didn't. I don't have any superpowers. All I have is this book. These words. And you might not know this yet, but words are *crazy* powerful.

Don't believe me? Then stop reading.

Put. The. Book. Down.

But do so at your own risk, because zombies are *real.* They're nasty, stumbling, slow walkers on a creeptastic mission: They want to eat your brainz!

Lucky for you, you're about to learn the secret. You're about to get a fresh dose of zombie kryptonite. Take it from a kid who came face to face with a whole nasty horde of the living dead on Halloween and...

Wait.

I'm getting ahead of myself. Ruining the "suspense."

You know, the scary stuff. The cliffhangers at the end of chapters that make your butt clench and keep you flipping the pages.

So, let me back up and start this story at the beginning. My first day at Haven Middle School. A normal school, really. Probably a lot like *your* school...

MONDAY

chapter 1

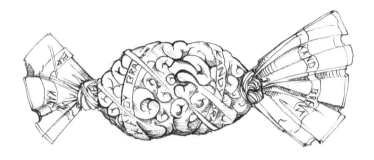

On the first day, I wasn't thinking about zombies. I was just riding along in Mom's blue van—a Honda I called the "Mystery Machine"—trying to read one of my favorite books.

And then Mom said: "Hey, Dash?"

She had her eyebrows arched, staring straight at me in the rearview mirror.

"What are you going to be for Halloween?"

"I'm twelve, Mom."

"But you love Halloween."

"I *loved* Halloween." I lifted the book high enough to cover my face.

"You used to come up with all those crazy stories for

your costume each year," Mom said. "Like when you were a ninja and made that cute papier-mâché sword."

"A *ninjatō*."

"What?"

"The sword, Mom. It's called a *ninjatō*."

Her eyes smiled in the rearview mirror. "It even sounds cute."

"Yeah," I grumbled. "*Cute*."

The Mystery Machine chugged down the road toward my new school. Mom and I didn't talk for a while. We didn't say anything about why we were *really* in Haven.

Dad's job.

How he works for "Kandy Brainz." It's this super-popular candy, shaped like a—you guessed it—*brain*. Dad doesn't care about candy or Halloween.

Dad's a salesman.

A *candy* salesman. And you know when the most candy is eaten, right? Of course you do. *Halloween*. The worst part about Dad's job is how every year, the week before Halloween, we have to move.

Every... stinkin'... *year*...

Kandy Brainz runs reports to find the *worst* Halloween towns in America. Like the places where kids eat the least candy. No trick-or-treating. No jack-o'-

lanterns. Every year we move to these super boring towns, and Dad breaks out all the Kandy Brainz swag—caps, t-shirts, thousands of sugar-filled brainz—and I hate it.

"*Dashiell Storey,*" Mom said with a tone that made me pull the book down from my face. "You still love Halloween. Just look at that book you're reading."

Halloween Tree by some dead dude named Ray Bradbury.

Busted.

I shoved the book down in my backpack. Through the van's window, I could see Haven Middle School taking shape in the distance.

"You think you're too old? That's it?" Mom said, the sharp tone gone from her voice. Back to being *Mom.* Cool and steady. My one constant throughout our gazillion yearly moves. "You're never too old for Halloween, Dash. You know better."

I stared through the window at my new school. Some of the kids were already out on the playground. The Mystery Machine was too far away for me to see any real details, but it didn't matter. Every year it was the same. The same lame school. The same lame town. All of it temporary until we had to move again the next year.

"Sixth graders don't go trick-or-treating," I mumbled. "Ask Dad. Sixth graders don't even eat Kandy Brainz. It's in the yearly reports."

"*Dash.*"

Mom's tone was different this time. Sad, maybe? She ran a hand through her red hair and sighed. She turned the music up on the van's stereo. Some dead hippie named Jimi Hendrix was singing like crazy. Mom's favorite. I asked her once what he looked like and she said: "He was a brain-melting guitar god with a wild afro."

Jimi's voice blasted out from the speakers: "I'm a voodoo child!" Mom bobbed her head and tried to sing along, but then she stopped and turned the volume down.

I felt bad.

"*If* I was going to dress up for Halloween," I said, watching through the Mystery Machine's windows as more of my new school came into focus. "*If* I wasn't twelve, fresh out of elementary school and almost a full nine weeks into sixth grade, then I *might* go as a-a—"

My mouth went all dry and nasty. I couldn't talk. I couldn't believe what I was seeing out on that playground.

Mom whipped her head around. "What, Dash? What is it?"

It was that word from earlier, that one I wasn't thinking about but now I couldn't help thinking about. I stared out at all my new classmates. It was like they were coming for me. Arms outstretched, drooling. I couldn't help it. I screamed—

chapter 2

"*Zombies!*"

Mom laughed out loud. "Maybe you should lay off the scary movies?"

My classmates had these weird goggles strapped to their faces. *That's* why I thought they were zombies. I was so busy watching them stumble around the playground, I didn't notice Mom leaning back over the console. I just felt her lips, wet and warm, as she planted a juicy kiss on my forehead.

"*Mom!* Gross!"

"I forgot," she said, smiling, blocking my view of

whatever was happening across Haven Middle School's early-morning recess. "You're twelve now. Way too old for *Mom* kisses."

I yanked the Mystery Machine's sliding door open and jumped out.

"And, Dash?" Mom said. "Please try and make at least *one* friend this year. Okay?" She paused, her eyes all squinty and serious. "It'll make Dad happy."

I slammed the door and watched as the van pulled slowly away.

Then I was alone.

Again.

In a new school, and this one seemed weirder than any of the other ones. A fog hung thick over the playground. A sign burned red through the morning: *Haven Middle School: Home of the Goblins.*

Goblins! Really? *Come on!*

Maybe I *should* lay off the scary movies. Nah. They weren't that scary anyway.

I started walking, but the other kids didn't notice me. They didn't even move. What *were* those things strapped to their faces?

Maybe this was like something out of a *Goosebumps* book, or maybe it was like *Coraline.* Maybe I'd crossed over into another dimension. I doubted if any of these kids had ever read those books, or even seen the movies.

Haven was the worst Halloween town in America last year. Then a thought came to me:

Hey, dork! (My inner voice likes to call me mean names.) *Maybe this won't be so bad.*

Maybe they'd just leave me alone. I remembered the book I'd shoved down in my backpack. *Halloween Tree.* Yeah, that sounded good. There were a few minutes left before recess was over, just enough time to escape into my own world.

I had the book in my hand, trying to find the page I'd bent down, and that's when I heard it:

Like a cell phone alarm or the sound a microwave makes when the chicky-nugz are finally done. All the students' headsets beeped at once. Their feet made crunching sounds on the blacktop as they moved into perfectly straight, single-file lines.

What?!

This was *sixth* grade. No more elementary school gar-bage. No more walking down the hall in lines. At my old school we had lockers. We had freedom. We could even chew gum!

The beeping stopped. The Haven kids just stood there. No roughhousing. No joking or laughing. *Nothing.* They weren't even talking.

Weird.

I tried to play it cool and started walking toward the

back of the line. I'd already looked at my schedule that morning during breakfast. Somebody named "Under-hill" was my homeroom teacher. Even the name sounded boring.

I kept my eyes down as I walked. My royal blue Converse All-Star Chuck Taylors ("Chucks" for short) were quiet across the blacktop. I was almost to the back of a line when a cold hand took hold of my wrist.

"And just what do you think you're doing?"

Even the guy's voice sounded nasty. His fingers were long like claws and freezing like ice. I looked up the man's arm to his face. It wasn't pretty. He had wild hair, all thin and wormy. Big dark circles under his eyes. And his teeth. They were butter yellow.

"I–I'm going to class," I said.

"Not before you tell me your name, young man."

"Dash," I said. "Dash Storey."

He nodded. "A new student, huh? I guess that explains the book in your hand."

I looked down and then up at this creepy teacher dude. "What's wrong with my book?"

His lips peeled back, revealing those nasty yellow teeth. "Books are not allowed at Haven Middle School."

"You're joking, right?" I said. "Why would books be outlawed at a *school?*"

In the distance, the students started marching toward the front doors. Slow, steady steps.

"You'll learn soon enough, Mr. Storey. Your homeroom teacher will go over all the rules."

The school doors snapped shut behind the students.

"Yeah," I muttered, feeling kinda sick, kinda scared. "I've got Mr. Underhill for homeroom. Maybe you could tell me where to find his class?"

"Sounds like you and I are going to get to know each other very well," he said and grinned.

I was so busy looking at his barf-colored teeth, I didn't notice his cold fingers snaking their way around my wrist again. He took my book—my favorite book!—and tossed it in the trash as he yanked me toward the school.

"*You're* Mr. Underhill?" I said and tried to pull away but his grip was too strong. "Where are you taking me?"

The smile melted from his face. He licked his thin, pale lips. "I'm taking you to my classroom, Mr. Storey. It's time to get you fitted for your headset."

chapter 3

THERE WASN'T a single picture in Mr. Underhill's classroom. Not even a motivational poster. You know, the
kind with some poor turtle flipped upside down and the
words, *Just keep tryin'*, written beneath the shell.

Mr. Underhill's classroom looked like a prison cell.
Four bare white walls. And all the kids still had those
goggles on. They were wearing them when I came in the
door. They kept them on as Mr. Underhill walked me
back toward the one open desk in class, sat me down,
and started explaining the rules:

"First off, the headset is your friend."

"A headset? What's a—"

He snapped his long fingers.

"I'm the one doing the talking here," Mr. Underhill said. "This is *my* classroom."

He bent down behind his desk and produced a pair of those weird goggle thingys all the kids had strapped to their faces.

"*This*," Mr. Underhill said, moving his hand like a magician, "is a headset. It's basically like a cell phone, or a tablet, but you wear it on your face and control it with your eyes."

Weird. Creepy. A combination of the two. Like something out of a sci-fi movie.

I looked around at the rest of the students. They were all just sitting there. Hands folded on their desks. Eyelids fluttering behind the flashing glass screens.

"It's the hottest new thing in education!" Mr. Underhill exclaimed, way too excited to be cool. He tugged hard at a strap on the headset. "And the best part? Students stay connected all the time. Your brain is always engaged."

"But—"

"But nothing," Mr. Underhill said, cutting me off. "It's technology at its finest, and these headsets are going to be Haven Middle School's secret weapon for the Zone One Marker Test."

"The what?"

"The Zone One Marker Test! It's only the biggest, most important standardized test in the country!" Mr. Underhill bobbed his head, his wild hair waving like seaweed. He kept yanking at the headset, clicking buttons, turning knobs, and then he started walking between the rows of desks, coming toward me. "Let's see. What else do I need to tell you? There's really not much, now that we have the headsets."

Underhill paused, studying my dome. He pulled the straps tighter.

"I already told you about books. There's no use for books at Haven. Not anymore. You have the whole world at the blink of an eye. Literally. Besides, books put too much stress on sixth graders' brains."

He stopped messing with the headset and studied my head.

"Ah. Bathroom breaks," he said and pointed to the door. "Only one student is allowed out of class at a time. That's pretty simple."

Mr. Underhill leaned over my desk, his long creepy fingers spread out, holding the straps of the headset. I tried to think of something, anything, I could say that would keep him from putting that thing on my head.

"Hey, uh–uh..." I stammered, and then it came to me: "When is this class over?"

Mr. Underhill stood up all at once.

Nailed it. He was speechless.

Except, his face. It was doing that creepy thing again like he was trying to smile but it was hard to tell because his teeth were yellow. Actually, now that I could see them up close, they were more green than yellow. Either way, Mr. Underhill seemed like he was *excited* about something.

"That's what I forgot!" He was way too happy about this. I felt sick again. "Because of the Zone One Marker Test, all students are staying with their homeroom teachers for the entire week. Five straight days of test-prep activities with yours truly!"

It was like the first part in a scary movie, when you know the hero should not go down in the basement... but then they do. Of course they do. And no matter how much you scream at the screen, you know you can't stop them. That's how I was feeling about sitting in Mr. Underhill's creeptastic class for the rest of the week.

"All right, Dash. Enough chitchat. Let's get you plugged in."

I looked up and saw Underhill's moldy hotdog fingers pushing the headset down toward my dome. He was so close I could smell his breath now. It smelled like a baby's poopy diaper.

"Wait!" I cried.

"It stings a little at first," Mr. Underhill said, grinning as he pushed the goggles over my eyes, "but you'll get used to it."

chapter 4

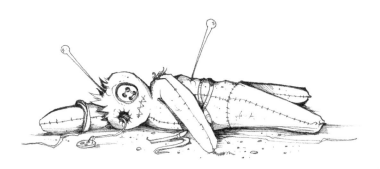

"*KEEP YOUR EYES CLOSED.*"

They *were* closed. I snapped them shut as soon as I felt the strap go tight on the back of my head. I wasn't stupid, and I did *not* trust Underhill. So, *yeah*. My eyes were closed.

But, wait, who said that?

"You hear me, kid? Keep your eyes closed or that thing will suck your brainz."

"Who–who said that?"

"*Shhhhhhhh.*"

The headset's little screen flashed in front of my eyelids. I waited a few more seconds, and then I whispered, "Who said that?"

"Better," the voice said. It sounded like a girl's voice, but I wasn't sure. "We don't want Underhill to hear us."

"Can I, like, take this thing off my head?"

"No way, kid. Underhill monitors everything. You can't see him right now, but he's probably got his legs propped up on his desk, his headset on, and—"

"Underhill wears a headset?"

"You gonna let me tell you the *real* rules or what, kid?"

Two problems: A) I didn't like being called a "kid." B) I was sick of *rules*.

I tried to play it cool anyway. "Underhill just told me all the rules, and they suck."

"Right," said the girl. I was sure she was a girl now. "And if you don't listen to me, that headset will *suck* your brainz right out of your head."

I could feel the headset whirring and buzzing, the way a laptop does when it gets hot.

"Like I was saying," the girl said. "Underhill is just sitting there. Probably playing DarkNite, like the rest of the class."

I wanted to ask about DarkNite, but I didn't want to interrupt this girl again. She reminded me of Mom when she said my full name. The same tone and everything. Not really mean, just serious.

"He won't get up all day," she said. "Nobody else will either."

"What the heck am *I* supposed to do all day? I can't even open my eyes?"

"Kid, are you listening to me? I'm trying to tell you how to *survive.*"

There was a long pause. I kept waiting as my headset flashed and buzzed. I took a deep breath and said, "Alright, I'm listening."

"You feel that?" she said.

At first, I didn't feel anything. Then I did. A warm hand on my arm. Much softer than Mr. Underhill's had been.

"Yeah. I feel it."

"That's me," she said. "That's real. Everything else in that headset, it's all fake. If you're going to survive Haven Middle School, you have to remember what's real and what's fake."

And then her hand was gone. I could still feel the place where her fingers had been. I got the chillies. The little blonde hairs on my arms stood straight up.

"Can you at least tell me your name?" I whispered.

Another long silence, then, finally, the girl said: "Izzy."

"You're a monorym?"

"A *what?*"

"A person with just one name. You know, like Beyoncé."

I thought I heard her laugh, but it was hard to be sure over my buzzing headset.

"My last name is Hendrix," she said. "Happy?"

"Like Jimi. That's cool."

"Who?"

"Jimi Hendrix, the brain-melting guitar god with a —" I caught myself before I went full weirdo. "Sorry. He's just some dead hippie my mom really likes."

"Never heard of him."

"No bigs. Didn't think you would."

"Because I'm a girl?"

"No," I said, quickly, trying to backtrack. "It's just that most kids my age don't like the stuff I do. I'm used to it."

She waited a while before she answered. I kinda hoped she might touch my arm again. It's nice to feel something warm, something soft, when you're stuck in the dark.

"What about voodoo?" she said.

"Like the creepy dolls with the needles and stuff?"

"Kinda," she whispered. "I'm from New Orleans. I know *all* about voodoo."

Okay. This was maybe the most *epic* girl I'd ever met. I wanted to know more.

"Since we have all day," I said, "why don't you tell me about voodoo?"

"Nope. Don't forget Underhill. He's sitting right there. Haven't you been listening?"

"You said—"

"He'll go for a bathroom break, eventually. He might hear us. Dude's gotta pee at some point."

I wanted to see this crazy-cool voodoo girl. I had an image of her in my head. I was just about to open my eyes and see if my imagination had the details right when she said: "Don't even think about it."

"What?"

"Opening your eyes. I'm telling you, Dash. You open your eyes and it's game *over*."

How did she know I was about to open my eyes? And my name! Did she just call me Dash? Was that part of voodoo? Maybe she was some sort of gypsy mind reader. Or maybe she'd just heard Mr. Underhill say it earlier.

"Listen, I'll tell you everything you need to know after school."

After school. Gross. It seemed like a lifetime away. It reminded me of when I was really little and my favorite TV show was *Scooby Doo*. I was totally obsessed with Scooby and Shaggy, the whole gang. Anyway, Mom liked to tell me how long something would take in "Scooby Doos." Each episode lasted thirty minutes.

I counted out the hours on my fingers and said, "That's like fifteen Scooby Doos."

Izzy said, "Scooby *whats?*" and I realized I'd just gone full weirdo.

"That's like seven more hours," I said, quickly. "What the heck am I supposed to do until then?"

"Sleep," Izzy said, her voice muffled now. "That's what I do every day. Just take me a big ol' nap, and then I play all night. It's awesome."

"*Sleep?*"

"Come on, kid. I already had my head down and everything."

I *was* tired. I'd stayed up too late watching *Ghostbusters* the night before, but I still had questions. "What if I have to pee? What about lunch?"

"Dash, just put your head down," she said, "and when you wake up, your first boring day at Haven Middle School will be over."

"And then you'll tell me all the cool stuff?"

"That's right," Izzy Hendrix said. "When the bell rings, I'll tell you all of Haven's dirty little secrets."

chapter 5

It was one of those dreams where I knew I was dreaming. You know? Like, you're flying—so, yeah, you *know* you're dreaming—but you can fly around wherever you want. Maybe over the top of Haven Middle School and drop watermelons on the blacktop just to watch them explode.

Epic.

I wasn't flying in this dream, though. I was still just sitting in class.

Mr. Underhill had a big red bowl cupped in his hands and a purple spoon. Like an oversized baby spoon. And what was down in that bowl, well, that's the part that made my stomach go all top-of-a-rollercoaster queasy. I put my hand over my mouth, afraid I was about to spew, and that's when the bell rang.

The end-of-the-day school bell sounded just like a dying cat: *Meee-ooo-www.*

All at once I remembered Izzy. Her voice rushed back into my head like I'd just chugged three Mountain Dews.

I scanned the classroom as the other kids took off their headsets and began plugging them into the chords dangling out from their desks. I saw a bunch of girls, but which one was Izzy Hendrix, the super-cool voodoo girl who knew all of Haven's secrets?

Izzy could've been any one of them. I didn't even know what she looked like.

The thought of going up to each of the girls, tapping them on the shoulder, and saying, "Hi, I'm Dash Storey. Do you know the secrets?" Or something. Maybe not those words exactly, but...

See.

This is why I don't have friends. Talking to other kids is not my specialty. Not at all.

I sat at my desk and waited for the class to clear out.

I plugged my headset in and everything. I was just trying to blend in, but this one kid, this tall, blonde boy with popsicle-blue eyes, stopped at the door and said, "School's over, new dude. It's time to go home."

I always chew my bottom lip when I get nervous. I bit it so hard I said, "*Ouch.*"

"What?"

"I said, '*Oh.*' You know, like, '*Oh, I forgot school was over.*'"

I chewed my lip and hoped the kid would leave me alone.

He laughed. That was good, right? Maybe he'd laugh his way right out the door.

Nope.

Now the kid was coming my way, and I could already tell from the way he was walking—this kid had swag. This was a *cool* kid.

"My name's Colt Taylor," he said and reached out his grownup-sized hand.

I looked from the hand to the kid and chewed my lip some more.

"What's your name?"

"Oh," I said. "I mean, wait. No. *Dash.* My name is Dash."

"Dash," he said and smiled. "Cool. Are you a bus-rider or a walker?"

Colt didn't even mention car riders. Maybe car riders weren't cool in Haven.

"*Boys*," Mr. Underhill said, looking up from behind his desk. "The day is over. It's time to go home."

"Checking on the new kid, Mr. U," Colt said. "You know, just trying to help out."

Mr. U? That was all I needed to hear to know Colt was a phony.

It was like this at every school. The cool kids wanted to look good. Everything from their fancy clothes, to their perfect smiles—it was all an act. Colt Taylor was just trying to earn brownie points in the crusty eyes of Mr. Underhill.

"I'm a walker," I lied, not wanting to look like a loser in front of this kid named after a baby horse. "I live in Coventry Pond Estates."

Colt nodded at Mr. Underhill, and that's when I saw it. Mr. Underhill *did* have a red bowl in his hands. The spoon was yellow—not purple—but he *was* eating something. Squiggly stuff. All twisted together and gross. My brain went wild, trying to guess what my creepy new teacher was eating.

"That's perfect," Colt said. "I live near Coventry Pond, too. We can walk home together."

I was already up, following Colt out the door, but I couldn't take my eyes off Mr. Underhill's red bowl. It was *so* gross. The way he just kept spooning pile after pile of those wormy squiggles into his mouth. They looked like—

"Brains!" Mr. Underhill burped. "Keep your brains good and ready for the Zone One Marker Test this Friday, boys."

Friday? Nobody told me the test was Friday. Halloween is Friday!

Wait. I'm twelve. I'm in sixth grade. I don't care about Halloween. *Right?*

"We'll be ready to go, Mr. Underhill," Colt said and gave our teacher a corny thumbs up. "We'll be back tomorrow and ready to learn!"

Was this kid serious? He sure acted like he was, waving at me, saying, "Come on, Dash. Let's go."

I looked back one more time at Underhill as he forced another spoonful into his mouth.

"Mr. Underhill?" I said, gnawing at my bottom lip. I couldn't help it. I *had* to know. "What are you eating?"

Underhill shoved his spoon down in his bowl, brought it up, and said, "This? Oh, you know, I'm carb-o-loading."

I had no idea what "carb-o-loading" was but it sounded super sketchy. I could see the squiggles up close now. They looked just like—

"*Ramen Noodles*," I said. "Oh…"

Mr. Underhill grinned and spooned another glob into his mouth. "They have tons of carbs. Keeps the brain healthy," he said, talking with his mouth wide open. "What did you think I was eating?"

chapter 6

THE WHOLE WALK HOME, Colt never shut up.

The way he talked was different now. He wasn't cussing or anything, but it was just *different*. It was so obvious he'd been trying to earn brownie points in front of Mr. Underhill. He wasn't even talking to me. Not really. He was just talking.

Mainly he talked about video games. DarkNite, especially. I remembered Izzy mentioning DarkNite. From what Colt was saying, DarkNite was basically just another survival action game. Except, it was made specifically for headsets. You ran around and tried to stay away from The Man In Black. Whatever. Video games aren't really my jam. There's nothing wrong with them. I'm just more of a book and movie kind of kid.

We walked down the sidewalk for a while. Haven looked like every other town I'd ever lived in. The school was mainly brick and the neighborhoods all had houses pressed in close to each other, green yards turning yellow as Halloween approached.

"So, yeah," Colt said. "That's all we ever do in class. Play DarkNite. I just hit level 82 today."

"Aren't there like firewalls or something?"

"The school's firewalls are stupid easy to hack. And Underhill never notices anything. He never even gets up from his desk."

"What about books?" I said.

Colt's face scrunched like somebody had snuck a stink bomb into his backpack. "Books?"

"Those things with pages?"

"I know what a book is," Colt snapped. "But nobody reads books anymore. They're, like, boring."

I nodded but decided to stop listening to anything else Colt Taylor had to say. I guess I hadn't really been listening that hard before. So much for making a friend like Mom and Dad wanted me to. It didn't stop Colt from talking, though. He just kept going and going and *going*...

Izzy Hendrix was my only hope. Where had she

gone? What did she even look like? I was imagining her face, her hair, when I saw the sign for Coventry Pond Estates up ahead.

It was a normal sign, like every other sign in every other boring neighborhood I'd lived in. But none of these houses even had pumpkins sitting on the front steps. No cobwebs or spooky lights. Definitely not any tombstones with zombie hands poking up from the ground.

Haven was quickly becoming the lamest town *ever*.

"See that house up there?" Colt said, pointing, but I didn't follow his finger. "That house is..."

Okay, so maybe I did follow his finger, and what I saw made me stop walking. The house he was pointing at was gnarly. Like scary in a way that wasn't fun. It stood two stories tall and leaned a little to the left. A dark house. With dark windows. Not a single light on in the whole freaky place. There weren't any jack-o'-lanterns or anything, but it didn't matter. It was just—creepy.

"Whatever you do," Colt said, and I tried not to listen, "don't go..."

That's when I saw it. In the top window. The darkest, tiniest window. A light came on. A *blue* light. And then, somebody—or some*thing*—stepped into the light.

I took off running.

Colt might have still been talking, but I didn't hear him. Nope. Nuh-uh, I was *gone*. My Chucks slapped hard against the road as I looked over my shoulder. Colt was just standing there, arms up and out. I looked past him. To the house. That glowing window. I could see a shadow now. The outline of a super-big head. An alien. No, that wasn't right. It was a—

chapter 7

"*GHOST!*" I screamed as I barreled through the front door of my house. "I just saw a—"

The look on Mom's face, it was like she'd seen what I'd just seen. Then I remembered she was supposed to pick me up from school today.

"Dashiell Storey, you're in big trouble, young man."

Trouble. I'd take trouble over whatever it was I saw in the window of that creepy house.

"Where were you?" Mom said.

"You'll never believe it," I said, ready to tell Mom all about the haunted house and the blue light in the window. "I was walking home and there was this house and—"

"Boo-yah!" shouted the heavyset man coming through the front door with the dark hair that looked a lot like mine, just a little shorter. "Daddy's *home!*"

Ughhh.

Don't get me wrong. I love my dad. We look almost identical: puppy-dog brown eyes behind thick black glasses, sharp faces like vampires, and larger than average ears. Except, Dad has this really big belly. Like a grownup-sized Dash ate a regular Dash. Or wait. Maybe Dad ate my brother and just hasn't been able to fully digest him yet! Wicked. I *am* an only child...

"Oh, babe," Dad said, talking to Mom, "Kandy Brainz is about to explode! I mean, the Havenites won't even know what hit them!"

Here we go. Dad's big progress report on how many sugar-filled brainz he was expecting to sell. This was *all* we ever talked about. Especially on the week before Halloween. I didn't want to hear it. I turned and started for the steps.

"Whoa, Dash-man," Dad said. "Where you going, bud?"

"Room."

"Not even gonna tell me and the Moms about your first day?"

I already had my foot on the first step, looking up the dark stairs toward my new room. The whole house was still pretty empty. A few family portraits hung in the living room. Three pumpkins were stuck to the fridge and two boney dudes hung above the stairs. Mom always tries really hard to make the new houses homey.

"You really want to hear about *my* day?" I said and turned to face Dad.

Too late.

He already had this life-sized (or maybe it was bigger than real life, I dunno) brain in his hands, holding it up for Mom to see. "This, *this* is going to be what saves our bacon this year, guys." Dad held the gigantor brain up like Simba in *The Lion King*. "Over one thousand calories, more sugar than *six* energy drinks, and it's the size of an actual human—"

"Uh-hmmm," Mom said, cutting Dad off before he busted out singing the Kandy Brainz theme song (*Kandy Brainz. Kandy Brainz. Eat one 'n you'll never be the same!*). "I think Dash was going to tell us about *his* day?"

"Forget it," I said and started up the steps.

"*Dashiell Storey*," Mom said with that sharp *Mom* tone again. "You're at least going to tell me where you went after school."

"What?" Dad said, turning to Mom. "You didn't pick him up?"

Mom put both hands on her hips. "Dash, I'm not asking you again."

I wanted to tell them both about how weird Haven Middle School was. How books were outlawed. How I'd slept all day and my teacher didn't even notice. Then I thought about telling them how I walked home with a friend, but that would've been a lie. And Dad would've gotten all excited about it. He might have even started munching on that humongo candy brain.

So I didn't say anything. I just shrugged my shoulders and turned back for the stairs.

"Nuh-uh," Mom huffed, pointing. "No sir. I'm *sending* you to your room, and when you decide to tell me where you went this afternoon, then—*maybe*—you can come back out."

"Cool," I said, already halfway up the steps. "I wanted to go to my room anyway."

chapter 8

SOOO UNCALLED FOR, *dork*. My inner voice, talking mean to me again.

But I guess I deserved it. I know Mom didn't. She was the cool one. Dad just *tried* to be cool, and that was worse. That's what bugged me so much. How our whole world revolved around Dad and Kandy Brainz. I couldn't stand them, anyway. The *Brainz*. They tasted like cherry-flavored cough drops.

Honestly, though, I did want to go to my room. My

room was my safe place, and I actually had it looking pretty wicked already.

I got to work as soon as The Mystery Machine pulled into Haven off I-40 last Saturday. I was like an unpacking robot. A *machine*. I knew exactly where my Baby Groot action figure went. Right beside Rocket Racoon. Duh.

All my rooms were basically the same, just like all the towns and all the neighborhoods and the schools.

My favorite horror movie posters went by the window. Super freaky villains stared down at me from the walls (each one a mind-bending creation from Eli Bones, the *best* horror director of all time). Action figures lined the floor. Black Panther. Captain Marvel. Iron Man. Posed and ready to defend!

I have all these notebooks I like to write creeptastic stories in, but I *never* let anybody see them. Not even Mom. The notebooks and the real books went on the shelf by the fish tank. Jawz, my travelling goldfish, *loves* to read. Or at least he likes to stare at the book covers. But he never seems too interested in my prized possession:

The flat screen Samsung LED forty-two-inch television I bought after saving my allowance for three straight summers. I always set it up at the end of my bed. That way I can curl up beneath the covers, have a book in my hands and watch one of my absolute favorite movies, all at the same time!

Who needs supper—who needs *friends*—when you have a room that's *this* wicked awesome? Not Dash Storey.

The Nightmare Before Christmas was already playing on the flat screen. I looked around for my *Halloween Tree* book. Then I remembered Underhill had chunked it in the trash. Didn't matter. I had books to spare. There were a hundred and seventeen books on the shelf beside Jawz.

I snatched one of my classic *Goosebumps* books —*Welcome to Dead House*—off the shelf and snuggled up under my Batman bed sheets.

Perfecto.

Just what I'd been waiting for, and I wasn't even tired. I could read all night long after the nap I'd had at school.

Jack Skellington was dancing and singing Christmas songs on the TV as I cracked open my creepy book. The house on the *Goosebumps* cover looked just like that house I saw on the walk home with Colt. A haunted-looking house with all the lights off—except one.

I slapped the book shut.

I was totally freaking myself out.

Get it together, Dash. Just read. That's what you do.

You're a reader. Read the pain away. Read until you can't remember moving to Haven, or how you don't have any friends. *Just read.*

Okay. Reading now. Not thinking at all about that blue light I saw in the window, or that extra-large head. Nope. Just reading about kids moving to a new weird town, meeting a bunch of wacked-out people.

Wait.

This sounded so stinking familiar.

I read faster.

Faster.

Time passed, page after page. I was so busy devouring this book, I almost didn't hear it:

A scratching sound at my window.

I peeked over page seventy-one. Had I really been reading that long? I checked the window. Nothing there. I checked the clock. It was a little past ten. I guess time flies when you're—

Another scratch! Louder this time.

I didn't want to look, but I had to. My eyes crawled toward the window, and I saw the same huge head with the blue glow from that creepy house.

It was hovering right outside my bedroom window!

chapter 9

I WAS ALL the way under my Batman covers. The Dark Knight would protect me. Right? Nothing bad can happen to a kid when he's under the covers. Nothing. Nope. Nada.

Tap. Tap. *Tap...*

I almost screamed. Almost. But if there really wasn't some ghoul hovering around outside my window, Mom—or worse, Dad—might hear me, and then they'd be marching up the stairs, and then I'd *really* be in trouble.

It was dark under the covers. And hot. I was trying not to move, trying not to breathe, when I heard a voice:

"Open the window. It's me, *Izzy.*"

Question: *How do you crawl out from under the covers and still look cool?*

Answer: *You don't.*

I threw the bed sheets back, opting for the fast-acting approach, and squirted out of the bed like MiraLAX when you haven't pooped in a week.

When I got the window open, I realized it was Izzy's hair that made her head look so big. She had this monster afro. Like how I imagined Jimi Hendrix. Except Izzy was alive and she wasn't wielding a funky-looking electric guitar.

"What-what," I stammered then got it all out: "What are you doing here?"

"Your room," she said, eyes scanning my posters, my books, landing on all those black and white composition notebooks with the stories I *never* showed anybody. "It's like—weird. What do you do with all those little notebooks?"

I ignored her question. "Izzy. What are you doing here?"

"You wanted to know the secrets, right?"

"Well, yeah, but it's ten o'clock already."

"New kid's got a bedtime," Izzy said, sliding back down the roof a little. "Okay... *Bye.*"

She was almost to the gutter. I had to say something. "How'd you get up here?"

Izzy stopped but didn't look back at me. "I flew."

I waited for her to laugh or something. Nothing. Just a crazy girl sitting on the edge of my roof.

"You—"

"I'm *joking*," Izzy said, scrambling back up toward my window. "I climbed up the drainpipe."

Oh, that explains it. She climbed up the *drainpipe.* Nothing to it. I wondered if my parents had heard her? I was too afraid to ask. So I said, "You live in that big haunted house?"

Izzy's head fell back and she laughed. Loud. *Way* too loud.

"Shhhhhhhh." I probably held my shush out a little too long, but if Izzy woke Mom up, things would go from bad to worse.

"Yeah, Dash, I stay in that big house on the corner of Coventry Drive. It's not haunted, though. It's just like really old."

"Haunted?" I laughed, nervously. "Of course it's not... *haunted.*"

"Listen, if you want to know the secrets. Like why you're probably thinking our school is so wack, then we got to go, like *now.*"

"*We?*"

"You're really going to make me spell this all out for you."

I looked over my shoulder to my Batman bed sheets. The posters. The dolls. I mean, wait—*action* figures. It didn't help I was already wearing my Avengers jammies. Izzy Hendrix most definitely thought I was a total dork by now.

"Okay," I said, turning back to face her. "I'll go with you, but I've got to get my shoes."

I tiptoed to my closet and grabbed my blue Chucks, but when I got back to the window, Izzy was gone. *Poof.* Just like that. I stuck my face out, eyes scanning left to right, and felt a hard slap on the back of my head.

"Come *on*," Izzy jeered.

She'd just scooted over to the side of the window where I couldn't see her. She slapped me on the head again, but not as hard this time. "I've got like *so* much stuff to show you."

I hiked my leg up, had it halfway out the window when I remembered I was afraid of heights. Like can't move a muscle when I look down over a ledge.

"You're killing me," Izzy said.

"Maybe you could just tell me the secrets here?"

"No way. Besides, I'm not *telling* you anything."

The way Izzy kept stringing me along, I couldn't help it... I put my other leg out the window. I was officially standing on my roof, twenty feet up in the air.

"This is a really big deal for me," I said. "I get

completely freaked out when it comes to heights, but here I am, out on the roof, just for you."

"Oh, *Dash*," Izzy said, super sarcastic. "You're my *hero*."

I rolled my eyes and when they finally focused again, Izzy was already sliding down the roof on her butt. "Wait up!" I snapped. "Aren't you at least going to tell me where we're going."

Right before she got to the gutter, Izzy paused and whispered, "Shadow Hills."

"Shadow *what?*"

"Shadow *Hills*," she said and then disappeared over the ledge.

I waited, my heart beating fast and low like a bass drum. I still wasn't sure what to make of "Shadow Hills," and then I heard her voice echoing back up through the drainpipe.

"It's Haven's oldest cemetery!"

chapter 10

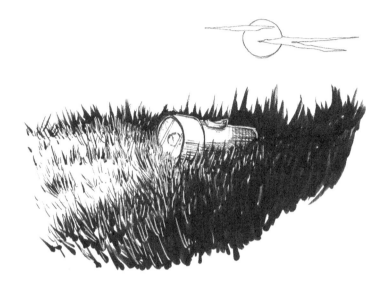

I SLITHERED my way down the drainpipe, my inner voice screaming: *OMG, OMG, OMG!*

When I hit the ground, Izzy was already running. She was fast. Like "The Flash" fast. Like a blur in the night fast. Like I could barely see her up ahead of me as I pumped my arms and churned my legs and wished I'd brought my inhaler... *fast.*

Coventry Pond Estates, apparently, was named "Coventry Pond" because there was an actual pond in the middle of the neighborhood. The streetlights ended where the pond began. Izzy zipped along the bank near the slimy green water, and kept right on going.

"Izzy!" I huffed. "Wait up!"

She turned around backwards, still running fast, faster than me. "Hurry up, dork."

It seemed like we ran forever, hopping fences, sprinting through backyards, ducking into the shadows when the security lights flashed on. I kept my head down. Tried to breathe in through my nose and out through my mouth like some coach told me to do once when I had to run the mile in P.E.

I kept putting one-foot-in-front-of-the-other, kept chugging along. And then I ran right into the back of Izzy Hendrix. We both hit the ground. *Hard.*

When I looked up, Shadow Hills Cemetery sprawled out in front of us in the pitch-black night. It was like something straight out of a freaktastic movie. The tombstones in ragged rows. Some crumbling. Some broken completely in half. Others were new with fresh mounds of dirt rising up in the dark. I was imagining boney hands reaching up out of the ground when Izzy said, "Okay, so, you wanted to know about voodoo, right?"

"Yeah," I said and shook my head, trying to snap myself out of the graveyard's spell. "Voodoo dolls. Pins and needles. All that stuff?"

Even in the pitch black, I could see the disappointment in Izzy's eyes. "I'm not talking about dolls, Dash. Like the ones you have in your room."

Burn.

She started walking, weaving her way around the graves, but talking over her shoulder. "I'm talking about way scarier stuff than voodoo dolls."

"Like?"

"The undead."

"You mean—"

Izzy stopped, turned, and flicked a flashlight on underneath her chin. Her face glowed campfire orange. "I'm talking about *zombies.*"

I have to admit, the idea of zombies was pretty creepy, but it wasn't all that believable. I mean, sure, I have a vivid imagination. I've seen things. Movies I probably should've never watched, like *Night of the Living Dead.* But I wasn't about to just go along with Izzy's idea that dead dudes were getting ready to spring up out of the ground. Nope. Dash Storey wasn't about to get freaked out for nothing.

So I tried to change the subject: "Is that a flashlight?"

Izzy's afro was awesome. It didn't even move when she shook her head. "I tell you about *zombies,* and you ask me about my flashlight?"

"It's just weird. I mean, what kid still carries a flashlight around? Where's your cell phone?"

Izzy huffed real loud like Mom does when Dad won't shut up about Kandy Brainz. She turned and started making her way through the cemetery again.

"I don't have a cell phone," she said. "My parents won't let me."

Finally. Me and Izzy Hendrix had something in common.

"Mine either," I said, walking a little faster, trying to catch up so we could talk about how stupid our parents were, but Izzy was like speed-walking or something. Apparently, she was a super-fast walker too.

"Dash, listen," she said, then stopped so quickly I almost ran into her again. "I'm about to show you something that's going to make you question *everything*."

"You're serious."

"Dead serious," Izzy said.

"Let me guess. This is like some YouTube prank where we whisper, '*darkness, darkness, darkness,*' and the bad guy from that DarkNite video game appears."

"You opened your eyes in the headset?" Izzy said and pointed the flashlight at me. "You played DarkNite? You saw The Man In Black?"

"Easy," I said, waving my hands in front of my face. "No. I just heard this one kid talking about DarkNite after school." I paused and took a deep breath. "I was just trying to be funny."

"This isn't funny, Dash," Izzy said and moved the flashlight so it wasn't in my eyes anymore. She worked it across the ground, the small circle of light revealing the dead grass, the dead leaves, the dirt where dead *people* were buried.

"You remember how I told you the headsets would suck your brainz out through your eyes?"

"*Yeah*," I said. "How could I forget?"

"I was lying."

I took a step back, expecting Izzy to start zombie-walking my way, arms out, going for my dome, but she just stood there with this super-serious look on her face.

"The headsets aren't actually going to eat your brainz," Izzy said and started moving the flashlight again, pushing the beam up the bottom of the tombstone closest to me. "The headsets are just like marinating your brain. Do you know what that means?"

"Like adding spices, making sure it tastes good. Yeah, I get it."

The flashlight's beam was dead center on the tombstone now, and what I saw was unbelievable. A name I recognized all too well...

chapter 11

"Our teacher..." I rasped. "He's *dead?*"

Izzy kept the beam on Mr. Underhill's name and took a step forward. "No, not really. The word we use in voodoo is *undead.* You know, like he can still walk and talk and stuff."

A flash of memories uploaded in my mind: Underhill's wormy hair, his nasty green teeth, his baby-diaper breath...

"I still don't believe you," I said, pointing. "It says 'Lonnie Underhill.' That could be his dad's grave or something. This in no way proves Mr. Underhill is a zombie." Even though I was talking tough, I was already taking a few steps back from the grave. "Come on, Izzy. Haven't you creeped me out enough for one night?"

I was just about to turn and start walking back to my house, already trying to decide if I'd climb the drainpipe or sneak in through the front door, when Izzy took hold of my wrist. Her hand was so warm, so soft.

"I'm trying to help you, Dash," she said. "Think about it. Think about *everything* that happened today."

I remembered taking a big nap. That was about it.

"Remember the Zone One Marker Test?" Izzy said, still holding my hand.

"What about it?"

"The Z.O.M. Test?" Izzy whispered. "Like *zom*bies. You don't think that's a little ironic?"

"No, it's not *ironic*," I said. "It's coincidental."

"And his name," Izzy said, completely ignoring me. "*Underhill*. The guy is literally buried under-a-hill. This cemetery is called 'Shadow Hills.' Remember?"

"So what?" I said. "Our teacher has a creepy name."

Izzy said, "Please, Dash. Just listen," and her fingers crawled down from my wrist and into my hand. "Mr. Underhill is using the headsets to make sure all the kids' brainz don't work too hard. He wants to keep them *ripe*."

I tried not to think about the fact that I was standing in a graveyard, holding a girl's hand. I tried to stay focused. "Yeah, ripe," I said. "Like bananas."

"Exactly." She squeezed my fingers like she was excited. "There's one thing zombies cannot stand, and that's when kids really *think*. It makes our brainz go sour or something."

"Did you go to some sort of voodoo school in New Orleans?"

"Dash, *please*," Izzy said, and now her fingers worked their way between mine. She moved the flashlight up so it was shining on both of our faces. "I'm telling you this because you're the only one who can save us."

I stared into Izzy Hendrix's deep black eyes. "Save *who*?"

"Everyone. The entire class," Izzy said. "You're our only hope because you have like a whole buttload of books. I saw them."

"Books? What do books have to do with this?"

She moved in closer and pointed the flashlight back at Underhill's grave. "Books make brainz taste bad, Dash. Don't you get it?"

As much as I liked holding this girl's hand, this was all too weird. I wriggled my fingers free and stepped back. "So you want me to try and get the other kids to read?"

She didn't move. She didn't have to. Her eyes said

what her mouth didn't. I couldn't believe it, but Izzy Hendrix might have even looked a little scared.

"No way," I said, shaking my head. "Nobody reads anymore. Especially not the kids at Haven Middle School. You should know that better than anybody, Izzy. Don't be stupid."

Her eyes shifted, turning down. It was the same look Mom had on the ride to school this morning. I instantly felt bad for being such a jerk.

I took a step forward. "Izzy, listen. I'm sorry for—"

"Shut up."

I blinked.

"Seriously, Dash. Listen," Izzy said, looking over my shoulder. "Did you hear that?"

A chill ran down my spine. I was suddenly aware of every sound in the graveyard: the croaking frogs, the wind whistling through the tombstones, the footsteps behind me.

The footsteps behind me?

I turned just as Izzy shouted, "Run!" and then my feet took over. Up. Down. *Up. Down.* My Chucks pounding through the cemetery. I glanced back just long enough to see a man standing on the hill in the distance. A tall man with a black hat, a black coat, and black tie. He wasn't running or anything, just standing there, covered in darkness.

Just as I remembered Colt telling me about the supervillain from the DarkNite game, I tripped, rolled, and crashed hard into an already broken tombstone. Izzy was still running up ahead of me, too far away to turn back now. My knees were all busted and scraped. I tried to roll over, tried to get back on my feet, and then I was hovering above the ground, my legs kicking in midair.

Two huge hands tightened around my shoulders like some sort of python death grip. I couldn't see his face—there were just shadows where his eyes and mouth should be—but I knew who he was...

The Man in Black!

TUESDAY

chapter 12

I COULD STILL FEEL his hands on my shoulders. Shaking me. I kept my eyes closed, waiting for The Man In Black to take me back to his evil lair, or whatever it was supervillains did when they snatched kids up from cemeteries.

"Easy, Dash-man. *Easy.*"

The voice was all wrong. And, come to think of it, he wasn't really shaking me that hard.

I opened my eyes.

"Dad?"

"Hey, bud." Dad grinned. "Bad dream?"

My Batman bed sheets were soaked. I felt my jammies. Did I just wet the bed? Nope. Whew. I was just sweating, and my knees hurt really bad.

"Yeah," I said, pulling the covers back. "A dream..."

"Must have been a doozy," Dad said.

I rolled over, put my feet on the floor, and stretched my arms out wide.

"Dash?" Dad said. "Why did you wear your shoes to bed?"

I looked down. My brand-new blue Chucks were covered in mud and grass.

"I-I don't know?"

"That's definitely strange," Dad said. "Maybe your feet just got cold. Anywho... Get dressed, little buddy, Daddy's driving you to school today."

The only thing weirder than me wearing my shoes in bed was Dad taking me to school.

"Where's Mom?"

"Still snoozing. She's not feeling one hundred percent this morning."

Mom—sick? Mom *never* got sick. Something was definitely up, but it gave me an idea.

"I–I'm not feeling good either," I said and coughed,

looking up at Dad with the saddest puppy-dog eyes you've ever seen.

He slapped me on the back. Hard. Dad was a big-time football player in high school. Quarterback. No. Wait. Linebacker. Maybe both? I don't remember. The only sport I've ever participated in is Taekwondo, and Dad says it's not even a real sport. Whatever.

"You know the rules, Dash-man," Dad said, talking like he was a coach and I was his star player, like it was the fourth quarter and we really needed to score. "The Storeys never take a day off. Not from work. Not from school. Not unless we're puking."

Come to think of it, my stomach really didn't feel that great. I put the back of my hand to my forehead like Mom would've done. Cold. Clammy. *Ugh*. No fever.

"I've already got breakfast fixed and ready downstairs," Dad said. "Get dressed, partner. Ten minutes and we're out the door."

The bed shook when Dad got up. I listened to him thud down the stairs, and my mind started spinning.

What really happened last night? Maybe it was a good thing Dad wasn't letting me stay home from school. I needed to talk to Izzy Hendrix.

I changed out of my jammies. They were dirty just like my kicks. And both my knees were speckled with bright red strawberries. Did I really go to the graveyard last night? Was what Izzy said true? And what about The Man In—

Nope. Not even going to *think* about him. Too creepy.

I had my blue and red Spiderman t-shirt on, feeling like Peter Parker. I was almost out the door when I remembered what Izzy had said. How she'd talked about all my books. How, maybe, they were the answer, like they could *save* the entire sixth grade or something.

"Jawz?"

When in doubt, always ask your pet goldfish for advice.

"You spend a lot of time staring all googly-eyed at my books. Which one do you think is the scariest? I need something that's going to *hook* them."

Jawz swam a fast circle like he was upset.

"Sorry, little guy," I said. "I should know better than to use a fishing metaphor around you."

He stopped swimming and came to the edge of his bowl, his big black eyes staring straight at my bookshelf now. At one book in particular.

"You're right! That's definitely the most creeptastic book I own!"

I snatched Jawz's favorite book off the shelf, just the one, and hustled out the door. After missing supper the night before, I was starving. I could only guess what Dad had ready for breakfast. He *never* cooks.

Halfway down the steps, the stench hit me square in the face. A dry, plastic smell I knew all too well...

Brain Tartz!

chapter 13

BRAIN TARTZ WERE Dad's company's attempt at breakfast food. Basically they were just these rectangular pastries with Kandy Brainz stuck all over them. They tasted like cardboard and cough drops. I snatched one up anyway on my way out the door. Like I said, I was hungry. Scratch that, I was *hangry*.

Dad was already waiting out in his company car. *The Brain-Mobile.* Despite having bloody brainz dripping all across the hood and the big loud *Kandy Brainz* logo stamped on the back window, his ride wasn't nearly as cool as Mom's Mystery Machine.

I crawled in the backseat and tried not to think about rolling up to my second day at Haven in *The Brain-Mobile*.

The first thing Dad said was: "Brain Tartz. Mmmm. The breakfast of champions."

He was trying to be funny, but it wasn't funny. Mom made the best PB&Js on the planet. I scarfed them for breakfast and lunch. But I knew I wouldn't be eating Mom's special sandwiches today. I didn't even have to check my backpack.

"So," Dad said, as The Brain-Mobile drove past Coventry Pond, "I think we should talk about last night."

Last night. There was no way I was talking to *Dad* about last night. He'd never understand. I looked past the pond. It didn't look nearly as creepy in the daylight. What about Shadow Hills Cemetery? Was there even such a place?

"I didn't come right out and say it this morning," Dad said. "But Mom, well, she's not really sick."

I wasn't listening. My brain was still running over the details of everything that had happened the night before.

"She's just really upset, Dash. She's worried about—"

Zombies.

The Man In Black.

"Dash-man? Are you listening?"

I crossed my arms and turned toward the window. We were getting close now. Back to my wacked-out school, Mr. Underhill, and all those brain-draining headsets.

"Mom's really worried," I snarled. "Yeah, I heard you."

"She's worried about *you*, Dash."

That got my arms unfolded. Got me to turn and face Dad. No more Mr. Tough Guy. Not when it came to Mom.

"Me?"

"She's afraid—" Dad paused and took a deep breath. I could see Haven Middle School out the window, all those kids and their headsets. "She's afraid our latest move has been really hard on you."

Hard on me? Are you kidding! Of *course* it's been hard on me. Every time we move it's like super hard on me. Try being the new kid at school every single *year!*

I didn't say any of that, though. I just kinda grunted and shrugged my shoulders as The Brain-Mobile stopped.

"So you're good?" Dad said. "There's nothing else we need to talk about?"

The way he said it, it was like he *really* meant it. Like he'd finally come out of his Kandy Brainz, sugar-induced coma and remembered he had a twelve-year old son.

I was about to open up to him. Spill my guts. Maybe even get the waterworks going, but then Dad blew it.

"You know, if you'd just try and make some friends..."

Game *over*. Power *down*.

Any shot we'd had at actually making a real connection was gone now. Dad's mouth kept moving, but I wasn't listening. Not anymore. It was the same old spiel anyway. He was back in *Coach* mode.

"There's nothing to it, Dash-man. Making friends is like selling candy. You have to—"

"Got it," I said and stepped out of the Brain-Mobile. "Thanks for the advice, *Dad*."

I turned and tried to slam the door hard enough to make a point, but the door didn't shut. It stopped half-way, just hovering there like it'd hit a force field or something.

"Now *that* is one sweet ride."

It wasn't a force field. Mr. Underhill had caught the

door before it shut. He was inspecting The Brain-Mobile, licking his lips like he was hungry.

"Yeah," Dad said and ran his hand across the steering wheel. "It's the company car. Kandy Brainz really knows how to make an impression."

"I'd say so," Mr. Underhill said, then ducked down and stuck his hand out for Dad. "I'm Dash's homeroom teacher. Lonnie Underhill."

Lonnie Underhill. That was the *exact* same name that was on the tombstone. First name. Last name. *Match.* Did that mean what Izzy had said was true? Was Mr. Underhill really—

"Nice to meet you," Dad said, shaking my zombie-teacher's cold, lifeless hand. "Dash has had nothing but great things to say about Haven."

That was a load of bologna sausages. I hadn't said anything about my teacher to Dad. I hadn't said anything about school to anyone besides Izzy. She was the only person who would listen.

"Ah, well, that's awfully good to hear," Mr. Underhill said, letting go of Dad's hand. "Dash has been a delectable addition to our class."

Did he just say what I think he said? *Delectable?* I glared past my freak-a-zoid teacher, waiting for Dad to realize Mr. Underhill had just called me, his only son, *delicious.* Like this kid's brainz are going to go great with some lima beans. But Dad just grinned, slapped the steering wheel, and said, "See ya later, Dash-man. Try and stay out of trouble!"

The Brain-Mobile drove away, and Mr. Underhill turned to me, grinning with his brain-munching teeth on full display. "Alright, *Dash-man*. Are you ready for your second day at Haven Middle School?"

chapter 14

READY OR NOT, I was back in Mr. Underhill's class as soon as the school bell (the one that sounded just like a dying cat) finished ringing. Same stuff, different day. All the kids were sitting there with their headsets on and buzzing. Just like they were yesterday.

I spotted Izzy on my way in. Her desk was right behind mine. She didn't look up. Didn't even move. Her headset was on, but I knew her eyes weren't open.

Maybe she hadn't heard me come in. Maybe she was too freaked from the night before to talk.

My headset was cold as I pulled the strap tight around the back of my head and pushed the big red power button. Bright lights flashed. I closed my eyes.

"Hey, dork."

"Izzy?"

"In the flesh. Did you bring the goods?"

I liked the way Izzy talked. I wondered if all kids from New Orleans talked like her.

"Yeah," I said. "I brought a book, if that's what you're asking."

"Just one? *Dash?* I told you to bring *all* of them."

I remembered running past Coventry Pond with Izzy. I remembered waking up wearing my Chucks with scrapes on my knees. I remembered the way it felt when The Man In Black grabbed me, the way he didn't have a face. Just shadows.

"Uh, Izzy?" I said. "What exactly happened last night?"

"Please tell me I'm not going to have to explain it all over again?"

I shook my head, then remembered Izzy's eyes were closed. "You don't have to explain anything, but I was wondering if you remembered the last part. You know, when The Man—"

"*Shhh*. Don't say his name out loud," Izzy hissed. "Not in class. He's chasing all those kids around through their headsets as we speak. That creeper might hear you."

So The Man In Black *was* real. And he could *hear* me? Freaky, but good to know.

"All that matters is you giving that book to somebody," Izzy said. "And since you only brought one, we're gonna have to be super smart about who we choose."

As soon as she said that last word, the desk in front of me rattled, and then I heard a voice I recognized: "Excuse me, uh, Mr. U?"

Colt Taylor. There was no mistaking a teacher's pet. After all the classrooms I'd been in over the last few years, I could spot a brown-noser with my eyes closed.

"May I go to the restroom?" Colt said.

See. *See.* Normal kids don't say, "*May I go to the restroom.*" Only brown-nosing teacher's pets say stuff like that.

"Sure, Colt," Mr. Underhill said. "But make it quick. You need to be studying for the Zone One Marker Test."

The desk in front of me jiggled again, followed by sneakers squeaking across the linoleum floor.

"*Dash,*" Izzy whispered. "This is your chance."

"You want me to give the only book I brought—my

most creeptastic, scare-your-hair-straight book—to Colt Taylor? No way!"

"Colt's the most popular kid in sixth grade."

"He's a brown-noser, Izzy. I thought you were smarter than that. Do you even know why they're called *brown-nosers*?"

For the first time since I'd known her, Izzy Hendrix didn't have some snarky clapback locked and loaded. She didn't say anything. It was perfect.

"A brown-noser," I said, proudly, "is called a 'brown-noser' because they're so busy kissing the teacher's butt their nose gets—"

"*Gross*," Izzy snapped. "I get it."

Two points: Dash Storey.

"It doesn't matter what you think about Colt," Izzy said. "Facts are facts: Colt is crazy popular, and if he starts reading books, *everyone* will start reading books."

"Right," I said. "But you know Underhill's stupid bathroom rule. Only one kid is allowed out of the class at a time."

Izzy stayed quiet for a few seconds, and that was cool with me. It didn't matter if I gave Colt Taylor my scariest book—I knew he was never going to read it.

"Dash, please," Izzy said and her voice sounded funny, like she was about to tell me another secret. "You have to give Colt that book."

I was just about to open my mouth, just about to remind her of Mr. Underhill's rule, when I felt her fingers slip their way into my hand.

"You have to do it," Izzy whispered, "for *me*."

Before I knew what I was doing, I was standing beside my desk. I glanced over at Underhill. His headset was pulled down over his eyes. He couldn't see me.

I squeezed Izzy's fingers—just hard enough to let her know I was doing this for her—and then I bolted for the door.

chapter 15

I closed the door behind me as quietly as possible. I'd made it! But there was just one problem—I had no clue where the bathroom was. I'd spent my entire first day sleeping. Remember?

I wandered down the winding halls, staring at the posters tacked to the walls. Four days until Halloween and there wasn't a single black cat, a witch, or a pumpkin, anywhere. Not even a scarecrow, or just some red and orange leaves. You know, like the schools that won't let you celebrate Halloween but will at least put up some "Fall" decorations.

Not Haven.

The only posters on the walls were about our upcoming test.

It's Almost Z.O.M. Test Time!

Or:

Use Your Brain or Lose Your Brain #ZOMTest

I felt like I was in some sort of dream. Like last night, except the halls just kept going and going. At least at Shadow Hills I could see the porch lights of the nearby houses. In the halls of Haven Middle School, there was just door after door after...

I couldn't help it—I had to see what was going on behind all those doors. I peeked through a window into one of the rooms.

What I saw was not what I was expecting. Not at all.

The kids were up and moving around. Working in small groups. And the teacher wasn't sitting behind her desk. She smiled as she worked her way from group to group. She looked nice, an older lady with cool red glasses.

What the *what?*

Where were the headsets?

I moved down to another door and glanced in the window. The scene inside was the same: happy kids, a cool-looking teacher, and nobody was wearing a brain-sucking headset!

I was headed toward door number three when a hand touched my shoulder. I jerked away and almost peed in my whitey-tighties.

"*Whoa,*" Izzy Hendrix laughed. "A little jumpy today, Dash?"

"What the French, toast!" I said and checked my pants. No pee spots. *Whew.* Close one. "I thought you were The Man In—"

"*Dash.* How many times am I going to have to tell you not to say his name?" Izzy leaned over past me, looking in the window at all the happy kids. "Weird, isn't it?"

"Why aren't they preparing for the Z.O.M. Test? Where are their headsets?"

Izzy touched the glass, pointing inside. "They're right there. Look closer."

I squinted and saw the headsets, one for every kid, still plugged into the desks.

"But they're not wearing them?"

"No duh," Izzy blurted. "Their teacher's not a zombie, Dash. It's just Underhill. Don't you remember? I showed you his grave and everything last night."

"How could I forget?"

Izzy took a few steps back from the window and turned to me. "Could've fooled me. I mean, I tell you that you're our only hope, that you need to bring enough books to save our whole class, and you just bring *one* stinking book?"

The book!

I'd left the book—our only hope—in my backpack! There was no way I was getting back into class and sneaking out again. I looked away, not wanting Izzy to see the truth in my eyes, and that's when I heard her laugh.

"It does look like a pretty cool book, though."

When I turned back, I saw that Izzy was holding my book in her hands.

"You–you have it?" I said. "But wait, how did you get past Underhill. How'd you get out of class?"

Izzy thumbed through the pages. She was wearing a flowery sun dress, but all the flowers were dead. Her afro looked even bigger than it did yesterday.

"I saw the book sticking out of your backpack and realized you'd forgotten it," Izzy said, grinning. "Then I told Underhill I was having a *girl* emergency. Need I say more?"

"No thanks," I snapped, reaching for the book. "I mean, *thanks*. I mean—wait—you're not actually having a 'girl emergency' are you?"

Izzy passed the book to me and rolled her deep brown, almost black eyes. "Our teacher is planning to eat our brainz on Friday, Dash. I'd call that an emergency."

"Right," I said and tucked the book under my arm. "So you really think Colt Taylor is the answer?"

Izzy nodded. "I do, but I'm not sure about this book? I mean, the title is kinda corny. That's the best you've got?"

I looked down at the cover of *Scary Stories to Tell in the Dark*. It was *Epic* with a capitol "E." There was this decaying head sprouting up from a hillside. It looked kinda like an evil clown smoking a corncob pipe.

"You don't think Colt will like it?" I said and looked up at Izzy.

She shrugged. "There's only one way to find out."

"Right," I sighed. "This is such a long shot, though. I don't even know where to find the bathroom."

"Next door on the right," Izzy said, pointing down the hall. "And you better hope Colt had to go number two, or he's probably already done by now."

I started walking toward the bathroom, still seriously doubting Colt Taylor was going to listen to me. "What if you helped me convince him?" I whispered over my shoulder. "You're like crazy confident, super cool, and that afro is the most amazing thing I've ever seen."

I waited a few seconds, but Izzy didn't say anything.

Smooth move, dork. Now she knows you like her. You definitely just beefed up your only shot at making a real friend.

I turned to face her. "I'm sorry, I—"

Izzy was gone. Like she'd just disappeared. The blood drained from my face and my fingers tingled. Footsteps echoed up from down the hall.

I clenched my jaw, walking backwards away from the click-clacking footsteps, and that's when I saw him.

The Man In Black.

He rounded the corner at the end of the hall and was coming straight for me. His face was all shadows, just like the night before.

I turned and ran. Made it three steps, still looking over my shoulder, and crashed hard into Colt Taylor as he stepped out of the bathroom. My book went skidding across the linoleum floor and stopped right beneath a pair of black combat boots.

Mr. Underhill bent down and lifted the book by the cover with two fingers, holding it out like it was a dead rat.

"Colt Taylor," Underhill said. "Of all my students, I never expected this out of *you.*"

"But–but—"

"Don't even try it, buddy," Mr. Underhill sneered and shook the book in Colt's face. "I'll now be escorting *both* of you to Principal Manson's office."

Mr. Underhill took both of us by the arms and we started walking. I was too scared to look back down the hall, too afraid I'd see The Man In Black again.

Come to think of it, the principal's office didn't sound that bad.

chapter 16

COLT WOULDN'T EVEN LOOK at me. For the entire thirty minutes we were waiting outside Principal Manson's office, he didn't say a single word.

His cheeks glowed red. There was sweat on his forehead. He was so mad I could feel the heat coming off his body.

But he wasn't the one who had lost his goldfish's

favorite book. That was two books Underhill had jacked from me now. *I* was the one that should've been peeved, but honestly, I was too scared.

"Hey, Colt?"

Nothing. He just kept sitting there, like a statue.

"I, uh, I didn't see you coming out of the bathroom and I wasn't looking because I was running already and —" I took a deep breath. "I'm really sorry. That's all I'm trying to say. I get diarrhea mouth when I'm nervous."

"*You're* nervous?" Colt hissed, coming to life. "I'm the one that's about to get royally busted."

Colt. Busted? What was he hiding? Did this kid have some sort of super-secret vaping habit? For once in my life, I kept my mouth shut and waited for Colt to tell me more.

"If Principal Manson checks my headset's history, my parents are going to ground me until I'm old enough to drive!"

"Because of DarkNite?"

"Yes, Dash. *Because of DarkNite.* We're not even supposed to play it at school, and it's like *all* I've been doing since we started reviewing for the stupid Z.O.M Test."

Ughhh. Not only was I never going to get Colt to read a book like Izzy wanted me to, I'd be lucky if he didn't try and beat my brainz in after school.

"All because of *you*," Colt groaned. "And to think, I was actually trying to be cool with you yesterday."

I wanted to ask if sucking up to our teacher and talking endlessly about leveling up in a video game was really what he considered being "cool," but I didn't get the chance. Principal Manson's door swung open, and I never could've guessed who was about to step out.

The Man In Black.

The air seemed to get cooler as he walked through the office. He was super tall. His footsteps sounded like hammer strikes. And then he was gone. Out the door. Maybe he didn't see me? Maybe he didn't want to blow his cover in front of the two secretary ladies and Principal Manson.

Wait.

Did this mean Principal Manson was in on it too?

One of the secretaries turned and looked straight at me, like she was reading my mind, the older, meaner looking one with the hair that glowed blue under the flickering, fluorescent lights.

"Dashiell Storey?" the blue-haired secretary said. "Principal Manson is ready to see you now."

I stood, glancing back at Colt Taylor. He had his head down, holding it with both hands. For some reason, I thought of my dad, the candy salesman. All his old school advice about how to make friends.

"*Hey,*" I whispered.

One of Colt's eyes peered up at me through a crack in his fingers.

"Whatever you do," I said, "don't admit to playing DarkNite. I got your back, *bro.*"

Maybe the "bro" was too much?

You're overthinking it, dork.

Whatever. I gave Colt Taylor a corny thumbs up, and walked slowly into Principal Manson's office.

chapter 17

PRINCIPAL MANSON's office was *not* what I was expecting.

The rainbow-colored wallpaper. The curvy pencils with the funky-shaped erasers in a mug on the desk. A puppy calendar tacked to the door, and *kittens*. Kittens everywhere! Not real-life kittens. Pictures of them. Like hundreds—maybe *thousands*—of cuddly kitty pics.

The total effect was nauseating. Like eating a whole

bag of Kandy Brainz then chugging a case of Mountain Dews. But I haven't even told you the weirdest part yet.

There was a clear glass nameplate sitting on the desk with big pink letters etched across the front. The name read: *Beverly Manson.*

For some reason, I thought my principal would be a man. Some freak-a-zoid like The Man In Black. I was wrong.

Principal Manson had short blonde hair cut just beneath her ears, golden hoop earrings, and she was *smiling* at me.

I almost turned and walked out the door, but then I remembered The Man In Black and Colt Taylor. How the coolest kid in sixth grade was currently super ticked because I'd just gotten him sent to the principal's office.

"Please," Principal Manson said, lifting a hand. "Sit down. I've been looking forward to meeting you, Mr. Storey."

I glanced over my shoulder as the office door swung shut. Wait! Was Principal Manson some sort of fairy-witch? That made sense. Maybe she was about to feed me a bunch of candy and then bake me in a kitty cake.

Before the door shut completely, I saw the blue-haired secretary's bony fingers on the handle.

Okay. So maybe Principal Manson wasn't a witch. *Maybe.*

I sat down.

"Dashiell Storey," she said and pulled a brown folder out from a desk drawer. "Do you know why you're here?"

I shrugged.

She waited, still smiling, and then said, "Let me try it a different way. How do you like my school?"

I *hated* it worse than any other school I'd ever attended.

Play it cool, dork. Tell her what she wants to hear.

"I, uh... I guess it's fine."

"I have your file here," she said, her tone flat now. "I see your family moves around a lot, don't they?"

"My dad—" I started, then stopped.

"Yes? Go on."

I took a deep breath.

"He–he works for this stupid company called Kandy Brainz, and every single year, the week before Halloween, we have to move to some lame new town..."

And then it was like some invisible dam broke inside me. My eyes got all watery. My throat went dry, and I told Principal Manson everything I'd never told anybody before. Not even Mom.

I told her how much I hated moving. How I never had time to make any real friends. I just kept talking, and

Principal Manson just kept sitting there, nodding her head like she was really listening.

Maybe that's why I told her so much. She was actually *listening* to me.

When I finished, Principal Manson sat back in her chair. That was it. She just sat back, breathed out, and kept looking straight at me.

"I–I'm sorry," I said.

"Sorry?" She leaned forward. "No, Dash. There's no need to apologize."

I wiped my nose with the back of my hand, and that's when I realized—if I wanted to rat out Mr. Underhill, if I wanted to tell this nice woman that she had a *zombie* teaching sixth grade—this was my chance.

Instead, I whispered, "W-What about the headscts?"

Principal Manson perked up. "The headsets? Do you like them? I mean, they're a great tool, but they can be overused. We've had issues with your classmates spending *way* too much time on unauthorized websites. We've tried every firewall, every content blocker, but I just can't keep them off of a video game called—"

"—*DarkNite*," I said and stared straight at her, my puppy-dog eyes fully engaged, trying to make sense of the pickle I was stuck in now: Either rat out Underhill or take the fall for Colt Taylor. If I took the fall for Colt, maybe then I could convince him to read a book.

"Yes," Principal Manson said, arching her eyebrows. "DarkNite is a *big* problem at Haven Middle School, but judging from your headset's history," she flipped through more pages in the brown folder on her desk, "you haven't logged into the server. Not once."

I swallowed, hoping my puppy-dog eyes were as cute as I thought they were.

"I–I've been using Colt's headset, Principal Manson." I sighed and looked down. Puppy-dog eyes disengaged. "Ours got mixed up yesterday, and I was too scared to tell Mr. Underhill. So whatever you see on Colt's headset history—it was all me."

When I looked up again, Principal Manson was staring at me, hard. Like maybe she wasn't buying it. Maybe she had backlogs of data. Maybe Colt had been playing DarkNite long before I ever arrived at Haven.

And then she tapped the brown folder and picked up the phone, bright pink fingernails clacking across the plastic buttons. She put the phone to her ear and said, "Yes, hello? Mrs. Storey? This is Beverly Manson. I'm the principal here at Haven Middle School."

Not cool. Not cool. So *not* cool. She could've at least told me before she called my mom!

"I'm so very sorry," Principal Manson said, "but I'm going to have to suspend Dash for the rest of the day and tomorrow. He's gotten into a bit of trouble with..."

She just kept talking, telling Mom everything, and then, I swear, she smiled. Just like she'd done while I was telling her all my deepest, darkest fears.

Maybe I was right all along. Maybe Principal Manson *was* some sort of fairy-witch. She'd definitely cast her spell on me.

chapter 18

NOT ONLY WAS I SUSPENDED, I was also *grounded*. And it was the worst kind of grounding. The kind where Mom didn't say how long. She just said, "Go to your room, Dash," as soon as we walked in the house. That was it. Sometimes, it's the stuff parents don't say that hurts the most.

Colt hadn't said anything to me either.

Not before Principal Manson called him back to her office. Not even when he came out and was sent back to class. He did look at me, though. This weird look, like he almost couldn't believe what I'd done.

Sitting up in my room, looking out the window, nothing made sense. I kept wondering what Izzy was doing at school. Did she even notice I was gone? Did

Colt tell her how I'd saved him? Had either one of them seen The Man In Black walking down the hall? Had *I* really seen him?

"You know what's funny, Jawz?"

Talking to your pet goldfish is one of the best ways to pass the time when you're grounded.

"I'm starting to think *I'm* the crazy one."

Jawz swam over to the edge of the glass. I wondered if fish had ears.

"Think about it, little dude," I said, looking back out the window. "I really and truly believe my teacher is a zombie."

A blocky yellow school bus hissed to a stop at the corner of Coventry Drive and Maple Street. Kids started pouring out. I scanned their faces for Izzy. Her haunted-looking house stood crooked and creepy just beyond the bus.

"And to make matters worse," I said, still talking to my goldfish. "I think I'm being chased by a—"

The bus pulled away and that's when I saw the long black car. My armpits instantly started dripping. The car drove slowly through the crowd of kids, letting them pass before it continued down Coventry Drive, heading straight for *my* house.

"Quiz time, Jawz." I put both hands on the window and leaned in so close my breath fogged the glass. "If you're a video game supervillain, one who wears a dark suit, a black tie, and has shadows for a face—what sort of car do you drive?"

The car pulled up along the curb in front of my house. I couldn't see through the windows because they were super dark. Of course they were.

"A black one!" I screeched, tired of waiting for Jawz to respond. "A black car would most definitely make sense for a freak-a-zoid that calls himself *The Man In BLACK!*"

The car door opened. My palms went clammy against the window. I could hear my own heart beating. Thump-thump. Thump-*thump*. A long leg emerged from all that darkness, then the dark suit jacket, and finally a head. A head with shadows for a face!

"Jawz!" I shrieked. "He–he's coming up the walkway. He's coming straight for—"

Boom. Boom. Boom.

The knocks on the front door rattled the whole house. I imagined him standing there on the porch with his shadow face. I pushed my forehead against the window, feeling a lot like Jawz probably felt, like I was trapped in a glass bowl.

Three more knocks. Louder this time.

And that's when I saw her.

"Jawz, look!" I yipped. "It's *Izzy!*"

She was standing in the middle of the road, staring up at my bedroom window. She was waving, frantically. Like she was telling me to *Come on!*

The window squeaked on its way up and my whole body went tight. What if The Man In Black had like super-sensitive hearing?

No time for conspiracy theories, dork!

Right, angry inner voice. You're *always* right.

And then I was out on the roof again. I looked back through the window just long enough to see Jawz swim down to the bottom of his bowl and hide behind the sunken treasure chest.

Smart move, buddy.

The roof shingles made crunching sounds beneath my blue Chucks. From the squeaking window, to my extra-loud footsteps, I knew I was making *way* too much noise. And climbing down the drainpipe would be anything but quiet. It was crazy, but I knew what I had to do.

I lifted one foot over the gutter, let it dangle there, and looked at Izzy.

She stopped waving, shaking her head, side-to-side. Like she was saying, *Nooo!*

I didn't have a choice. The Man In Black was probably already coming up the steps by now. I held my breath, closed my eyes, and then I jumped.

chapter 19

THE AIR WENT OUT of me all at once. One big *whoosh*.

Luckily, I landed in one of the huge rose bushes in front of our house. I fought to breathe, slapping at the bush's thorny limbs, spitting out leaves and dirt. I could only imagine the amount of noise I was making. So much for my stealthy escape.

I peeked through the bush in time to see the front door slam shut. Wait. What about—

Mom?

I was just about to storm the porch and burst through the front door (maybe my Taekwondo lessons would finally pay off) when a warm hand slipped through the roses and took hold of my shirt collar.

"*Dash,*" Izzy whispered. "How are you not dead?"

"The Man In—" I rasped, but Izzy clamped her hand over my mouth.

I jerked away, snarling, "He's got my *mom,* Izzy. I have to go back in there."

"No way," she said. "Besides, you don't have anything to worry about."

"But, that's my—"

"You've really never played DarkNite before, have you?"

I shook my head.

"The Man In Black can only hurt kids," Izzy explained. "His powers are completely useless when it comes to adults."

My chest rose and fell. I was breathing so hard, adrenaline coursing through my veins after my leap of faith, I could barely think straight.

"Wh-what are we going to do?" I said, finally.

Izzy stepped back out of the rose bushes and tugged on my shirt. "We can't stay here. I know that much."

I stepped out of the bushes. The fall air tasted like campfire smoke and dead leaves.

"What about your house?" I tried. "Maybe we could hide out there."

Izzy shook her head, quick. Almost *too* quick. Like she was hiding something.

"Think about it," she said. "He knows we're in the same class."

"Okay, yeah, but like half our class lives in Coventry Pond Estates."

"I don't have time to argue with you, Dash."

Izzy's tone was different than I'd ever heard from her before. She turned, took one step, and then she started to run.

"*Wait*," I pleaded, realizing my house's front door was the only thing separating me from another encounter with The Man In Black. "Where are you going?"

Izzy didn't even turn. She just shouted into the crisp fall air: "I'm going to the last place that creeper will ever look." She kept running, getting farther and farther away. "Are you coming or what?"

chapter 20

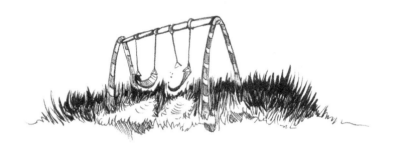

I FOLLOWED Izzy as she cut back behind Coventry Pond again, our shoes sinking down in the soft mud by the bank. Then we weaved across downtown, through the Walmart parking lot, and by the time we reached the school, the sun was almost down.

Long shadows played out across the playground. Everything looked different in the dusky light.

"S-S-*School*?" I finally managed to get the word out, both hands on my knees, trying hard to catch my breath. "This was your big plan? Come back to school? I don't get it."

Izzy jerked on the front door. Locked. She let out a string of words that would've definitely gotten her suspended if there had still been teachers around to hear her. The glass rattled when Izzy slapped the door, and then she took off running again.

"Wait," I groaned. "Where are you going now?"

Izzy's feet thudded to a stop. "We've got to get inside."

"You don't think we could just hide out on the playground somewhere?"

"I'm sure The Man In Black will never see you hiding under the slide, Dash."

I was so busy trying to decide if Izzy was being sarcastic, I didn't see her take off running again. When I looked up, she was almost around the edge of the school, almost out of sight.

"You know the school's locked. It's *always* locked!" I shouted. "Every school I've ever been to stays locked up like a prison."

Izzy glanced back over her shoulder.

"There's always a chance, Dash. One of the night janitors could have a door propped open, or one of the teachers might have left their window unlocked."

I nodded and took a few steps toward her. I couldn't get over how the school seemed even freakier without any kids around.

"Okay," I said. "Maybe we could get into the school, but you've got to tell me—what are we going to do once we're in there?"

Izzy's jaw flared as she jabbed both hands onto her hips. "What makes you think I have to tell *you* anything, Dash Storey?"

Good point. Maybe it wasn't smart to tick off a voodoo girl that lived in a haunted house.

"It's your fault we're here anyway," she snapped.

"*My* fault?"

"If you would've just done like I told you and brought all your super-nerd books to school..." My inner voice screamed: *Super-nerd?!* "...then we wouldn't have to be busting into the school so we can break all the headsets."

I was so stuck on the super-nerd thing (my books were *not* nerdy) it took a moment for Izzy's words to sink in.

"Wait!" I barked as what she'd said finally penetrated my skull. "Did you just say we're going to *break* all the headsets?"

"Yeah, dork. Come on," Izzy said, already trotting around the corner of the school. "There's only one teacher dumb enough to leave a window unlocked."

"Yeah?" I said, jogging along behind her. "Who?"

"You know who."

Underhill.

I didn't even have to say his name. When I looked

up, we were standing right outside Mr. Underhill's window, so close we could reach out and touch it.

"*Izzy*," I whispered. "I'm not so sure this is a good idea. The school has security cameras. I really don't want to get suspended again."

She put a finger over her lips and turned, slowly, to face the window.

The brick was warm on my back. I tried to steady my breathing. I couldn't see in the window so I watched Izzy's eyes instead, growing wider and wider.

"*Dash*," she said, motioning for me with her hand. "You've got to see this."

Nuh-uh. No way. Whatever was waiting for me on the other side of that glass—I didn't want to see it.

Izzy's hand shot out and took hold of mine again, just like she'd done in the cemetery. But it wasn't working this time. Nope. I was *not* letting Izzy Hendrix drag me in front of that window.

And then she did.

One swift jerk of her arm, and I was standing right there beside her.

At first, I didn't see anything. It just looked like our classroom. The bare, white walls. All the desks in rows. Except the lights were off. No bigs. I breathed a sigh of relief.

"You see him?" Izzy whispered, pointing.

In the corner closest to us, a computer screen glowed. The dim light was just enough to reveal Mr. Underhill sitting behind his desk, headset on, munching away on what looked like a big plate of—

"*No way*," I rasped and jerked free of Izzy's hold, pressing my back against the wall again. "What's he eating?"

"I told you, Dash. I *told* you he was a zombie."

I peeked back around the window, just far enough I could see Underhill. Whatever he was eating, it wasn't Ramen Noodles. It looked like a big gray blob. It jiggled a little every time he stabbed it with his fork.

"*Please*, Izzy. Let's go."

She just kept standing there, watching as Underhill forked a lump of the gray stuff off his plate and into his mouth.

"Izzy," I cried, taking a step back from the window but keeping my eyes on my brain-eating teacher. "There's no way we're getting in there. Let's *go!*"

Izzy whipped her head around and screamed with her eyes: *Waaay too loud, dork!*

Mr. Underhill's fork stopped before it reached his mouth. It hovered there as he lifted the headset up from his eyes with his other hand.

I was too scared to move. Izzy wasn't budging either. We were both frozen, hoping Underhill would just go on eating his brainz and not notice us standing right outside his window.

His eyes scanned left to right, and then, all at once, he jerked his head toward the window like he'd known we were watching him all along.

"Run!" Izzy blurted.

I felt her bolt past me. Heard her feet stomping through the grass. But I couldn't move. My legs wouldn't work, and Underhill was standing up now, coming straight for me!

chapter 21

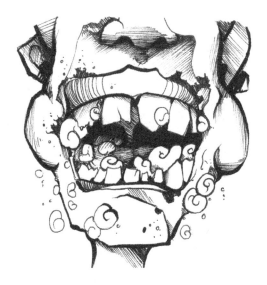

RIGHT BEFORE HE got to the window, my legs came to life.

I jumped like actors do in movies when a car explodes in the background, diving away just as I heard the window slide open.

Underhill stuck his head out, still holding his plate with one hand as he peered out across the playground.

I kept squatting there, less than five feet away from a real-life zombie, my heart beating so hard, so fast, I *knew* he would hear it.

"That's strange," Underhill mumbled to himself.

I closed my eyes, but I could still hear him breathing, wet, ragged sounds like Dad makes sometimes when he's snoring, followed by a crunch, crunch, *crunch*.

Gross!

I could actually *hear* him munching the brainz! I had to get out of there.

Down on all fours, I crawled my way along the edge of the school. When I made it to the corner, I stood and ran.

"Hey!" Mr. Underhill shouted. "Hey, you, come back here!"

Not a chance! I ran my life depended on it, because, honestly, I guess it did.

I cut back through the Walmart parking lot and made it all the way to Coventry Pond before my throat clenched and I had to stop running. My chest burned. I wheezed and wished so bad for my inhaler. After a few more steps, I made it past the pond and could finally see my house.

We hadn't lived in Haven long enough for it to actually feel like *home*, but I'm not gonna lie, seeing the warm lights in the windows, imagining Mom in there with supper ready—it felt pretty good.

And the best part: The Brain-Mobile and The

Mystery Machine were parked out front, but that was it. The Man In Black's creepy car was gone!

Whew. What a day.

I thought about climbing up the drainpipe, sneaking back into my room, and hoping my parents hadn't realized I was gone, but I was *so* tired.

What'd it matter, anyway? I was already grounded.

The front porch steps creaked beneath my weight. I pushed the front door open, took one step inside, and then I saw Mom and Dad. They were both just sitting in the living room. Dad had his armed wrapped around Mom's back. Her face was pressed tight against his shoulder.

When Mom looked up, there were lines of black mascara running down her cheeks.

"*Dash,*" she cried, standing up and coming for me. "Oh, Dash."

Her voice didn't sound angry, and Dad just kept sitting on the sofa.

None of it made sense.

Mom took me in her arms and squeezed me tight. She was warm and smelled like peanut butter.

"We've been so worried about you," Mom whispered. "So worried, but everything's going to be okay now. Everything's going to—"

A toilet flushed somewhere in the house. It seemed

weird, a toilet flushing while everyone was still in the living room. Wait. *Who just flushed the toilet?*

Down the hall, the bathroom door creaked open. I could only see a hand at first. A ginormous hand.

And then a long, dark arm.

And then a suit jacket—an all *black* jacket.

chapter 22

THE MAN IN Black made his way down the hall, past my dad still sitting on the couch, and walked straight up to me. The whole room went cold, and then, I swear, the lights flickered.

I tried to turn and run, but Mom was still hugging me. She clamped down harder when I tried to jerk away.

It was a trap!

How could my very own parents do this to me?

I held tight to Mom and glanced up at The Man In Black.

He looked different up close. I could finally see his face. It was covered with black beard stubble, a "five o'clock shadow," like Dad gets sometimes when he doesn't shave on the weekends. Okay, so maybe I'd just been imagining the freaky shadow face. *Maybe...*

"Dash?" Mom said, pulling back. "Your father and I think this is best."

"*Mom*," I cried. "Wh-what did I do?"

The Man In Black stepped forward, holding out his humongous hand. "It's more like what you haven't done, Dash."

I looked from the man's hand back to Mom. Dad still hadn't moved from the sofa.

"So, what? You're just handing me over to this *monster!*" I shrieked.

"Monster?" Mom said and glanced back at Dad. He shrugged his shoulders. "This is Special Agent Frank Black. He's here to help, Dash."

Special Agent? That didn't explain anything. For all I knew, there were more creepy dudes in suits waiting out in his black sedan.

Agent Black (*if* that's really his name) just kept holding his hand out, like he wanted me to shake it.

"I'm here to help *you*, Dash." His voice was really low, like thunder. "I think I can explain some of the problems you've been having at Haven Middle School."

Problems? Like the fact that I have a *zombie* for a teacher?

"*Dash*," Mom snapped. "Shake Agent Black's hand."

I grunted and reached out. His monster hand engulfed mine, but he was gentle. He didn't squeeze too hard like other grownups did.

"I really am here to help," Agent Black said, still shaking my hand, "if you'll just let me."

We both let go at the same time. He kept looking at me, though, like he was waiting for me to speak.

"Whatever," I said, and looked at Mom. "I guess that's fine."

Mom pressed both of her hands together and Dad finally got up from the sofa. Together, they started walking away.

"Uh, wait. What's going on?" I said.

I watched as Mom and Dad disappeared into the kitchen

"You and me, Dash," Agent Black said. "We need to talk, *alone.*"

chapter 23

THE SOFTNESS of Agent Black's handshake carried over into our conversation. The first thing I asked him was where he'd parked his car. He said he'd had to move it around back. Mom was afraid he'd get a ticket parked on the curb. He really seemed like a good guy. Come to find out, he was a "Special Agent" with the Z.B.I.

The *Zombie Bureau of Investigation.*

I was liking this guy more by the second.

"So, you're like a Ghostbuster?" I said, unable to keep my nerd love on the down low. "That. Is. AWESOME!"

Agent Black shook his head. "No, I'm not a *Ghost-buster,* Dashiell. Well, not really..."

"See. *See!* I knew it!"

"I mean, yes, sure, I keep watch over the undead, but ghosts are never really the problem."

"*Zombies!*" I almost shouted. "Just like Mr. Underhill!"

"That's who I'd like to talk to you about."

I sprang up from the sofa and started pacing. Agent Black kept his cool, staying seated in Dad's faded La-Z-Boy, rocking slowly back and forth.

"Listen, I'll tell you everything," I said, excitedly. "Just this afternoon, like right before I got here, I saw the dude eating *brainz*. A whole plate of them. He was even using a fork, which I thought was kinda weird."

"A fork, huh? That is strange." Agent Black nodded. "But that's not the sort of information I'm looking for."

I stopped pacing, standing by the door that led to the kitchen. I wondered if Mom and Dad were back there, listening in on our conversation. If they were, what were they thinking? Had Agent Black already told them about my zombie teacher?

"I'm interested in the headsets," Agent Black said. "This is new technology. We've never seen it used the way Mr. Underhill is using it."

"So what Izzy said was true?"

"*Izzy?*" Agent Black asked. "Who's Izzy?"

Maybe I'd said too much. Maybe I shouldn't be

getting my only real friend mixed up in this craziness. I tried to change the subject: "So you're saying, Underhill really *is* using the headsets to keep our brainz fresh?"

"Fresh isn't really the right word."

I raised both of my eyebrows at the Special Agent.

"Flavorful would be more accurate," he said. "See, you have to remember zombies are dead. Their taste buds are different than humans."

I hadn't realized zombies even had taste buds.

"They like to eat stuff that's decaying, stuff that's rotten," he said. "It adds flavor."

"So the headsets really are hurting the students' brainz?"

Agent Black breathed in deep. His shoulders rose and fell. "According to our studies, when adolescent brains are exposed to headsets for long periods of time, there's a rapid decline in cognitive ability."

"Uh?" I groaned. "English please."

Agent Black actually looked embarrassed. "Basically, headsets aren't good for kids, especially when they use them too much."

"Got it." I walked back over to the sofa and sat down across from Agent Black. "But the kids don't really get to wear them that much at our school. Like even in Underhill's class, they're only using them a bunch right now because of the Z.O.M. Test."

"Exactly," Agent Black said and leaned forward. "The Z.O.M. Test is Underhill's excuse for abusing the headsets. And the way he's letting the kids play DarkNite all day—that's his secret weapon."

"You—you know about DarkNite?"

Agent Black pulled a cell phone out from his suit jacket and turned the screen so I could see it.

"What's that?" I said, trying to make sense of all the colors and numbers.

"It's a map that shows the areas where kids are playing the most video games," he said. "DarkNite just came out this year, but it's quickly become the new favorite."

I squinted and could just make out Haven on the map. The town was completely red. My eyes scanned down to the map key: *Red = 90% Infected.*

"Infected?" I murmured. "What does that mean?"

Agent Black clicked the screen off and stood. Dad's La-Z-Boy rocked to a stop behind him. "I know I told you I came here to help you, Dash," he said, walking slowly toward the door, "but that wasn't really the truth."

Sitting on the sofa, my left knee started to bounce. I bit down on my bottom lip.

"The truth is, almost every one of your classmates is addicted to DarkNite." Agent Black stopped at the front door and turned to face me. "And the worst part, Dark-Nite is a Zom-Corp product. It's still so new, we don't know much about it."

"You–you mean," my knee was going bonkers now, "DarkNite is *made* by zombies."

"Bingo." Agent Black nodded. "And, Dash, if we don't stop these kids from playing that game by Friday, we might never see them again."

I stood up fast. Too fast. My head felt all light and woozy.

"Friday?" I mumbled. "So that part really is true? Underhill's planning to eat our brainz on Halloween, like while we take the Z.O.M. Test?"

Agent Black's dark eyes narrowed. "You knew that already?"

Izzy was the one that had told me the truth about the Z.O.M. Test, but I was supposed to be keeping Izzy *out* of this. I chewed my bottom lip and tried to cover my tracks.

"Uh, wait. You said 'we' just a second ago. 'If *we* don't stop the kids from playing DarkNite.' Those were your exact words. Are you talking about you and the other Special Agents?"

He shook his head, slowly. "This is a classified mission, Dash. There are no other agents. It's just me and you."

"*Me?*" I rasped. "How am I supposed to help you?"

"I'm about to tell you something you can't tell anyone." Agent Black glanced over my head to the kitchen. "Not even your parents."

"Do they know about this? About the zombies and the—"

"It's *classified*, Dash. Top secret. That means you can't tell *anyone*."

I gnawed on my lip, trying to guess what Agent Black was about to say next.

"I want you to go undercover," he said, reaching out for the doorknob and turning it. "Tomorrow morning. I want you to go back to school, put on one of those headsets, and then report back to me in the afternoon."

"But the headsets are—"

"I'll be close by, Dash. You don't have anything to worry about."

Agent Black opened the door and stepped onto the front porch.

"And just what, exactly, do you want me to do?" I bit down on my lip so hard I tasted blood.

Agent Black finally stopped walking, turning back to me now.

"I want you," he said, his face all shadowy again, "to *play* DarkNite."

WEDNESDAY

chapter 24

WHEN MY HEADSET CLICKED ON, it felt like worms were crawling around inside my brain. Like a million tiny ants, marching through my eyes and into my skull.

Wait.

If this book really is going to save your life, I have to get every detail right. I better back up. I can't leave anything out.

I couldn't sleep the night before. I kept hearing Agent Black's voice, kept worrying about my *classified* mission.

To tell the parents, or not to tell the parents: that is the question.

Or at least that's the question I kept asking myself, the one I still couldn't answer when Mom drove me to school in the morning.

I knew Mom wanted to ask me stuff about Agent Black, but she didn't. Mom's cool like that. Maybe she knew words couldn't really cover the kind of crazy we were up against now. Or maybe she was just too scared to talk about it.

The nervous tension was so thick you could've cut it with a butter knife. I tried to think of something to say, something pointless that would just get our mouths moving.

"Uh, Mom?" I mumbled. "How are things going with Kandy Brainz?"

Mom probably knew I didn't care about Dad's job, but she played along anyway.

"Dad's worried, Dash. Things are different this year."

I'd never seen Dad worry about anything before. He always hits his quota by Halloween.

"Your father's really having a tough time selling candy in Haven. None of his old tricks are working."

"What about that gigantor brain thing he had the other night? The kids aren't buying that?"

Mom shook her head. "They're not buying anything, Dash. It's like they've all been brainwashed."

Had Mom overhead what Agent Black told me last night? Was she pulling her patented "Mom" move, the one where she talked around a subject and squeezed a confession out of me before I even knew what had happened?

"It's all so strange," Mom said as the Mystery Machine pulled up in front of school. "Your dad just can't figure out what to do."

I leaned over the van's console and kissed Mom on the cheek. Right there in front of the other kids and everything. I didn't care what anybody thought. Not anymore.

Dash Storey was on a mission.

Not only was I going to get some super-secret recon on DarkNite for Special Agent Frank Black, but I was also going to save my dad's job.

The van door slammed and Mom drove away. I didn't wait for Mr. Underhill to come find me and say something creepy. I just turned and started trotting into the school, heading straight for class.

There was only one person I wanted to see. I knew I couldn't tell her everything. Actually, I couldn't tell her *anything*. But still, Izzy Hendrix was my best friend. My *only* friend. And it would sure be nice to see her before I strapped my headset on and started my super-secret Z.B.I. mission.

But nobody was in class when I got there.

I kept waiting, and then the bell rang. The students marched down the hall in their perfectly straight lines. Most of them were already wearing their headsets. Mr. Underhill was out front, leading them along like a pack of blind rats.

There was something different about him today, though. He didn't smile at me or make some snarky comment. He just unlocked the door and walked into class.

I sat down at my desk, unplugged my headset, and kept hoping I'd see Izzy.

Colt Taylor glared at me on his way in. I ignored him.

"Today is Wednesday," Mr. Underhill groaned. "That means you kids only have two days to prepare for the Zone One Marker Test."

His voice was different too, almost shaky, like he was sick or something.

"It is very important that you make the most of these next two days." I kept trying to figure out what was different about Underhill's voice. "Keep your headsets on, and do *not* take them off."

Then it hit me like a dodgeball in P.E. class: Underhill sounded *hungry*. Like he was *starving*!

I glanced around the classroom as the few students who weren't already wearing their headsets put them on and pulled the strap tight in the back.

Where the heck was Izzy?

I tried to remember the night before: both of us running away from the school, running while Mr. Underhill stood at the window, calling for us as he sprayed brain-bits out of his mouth.

Had Izzy made it home? Was she safe?

"Excuse me?" Mr. Underhill's voice shook me from the memory. "Have I not made myself clear, Dash?"

"No. I mean, wait. *Yes—*"

Mr. Underhill propped his feet up on his desk, his wormy yellow hair swaying in the breeze blowing out of the air conditioner.

"Would you like to take another trip to go see Principal Manson?"

I said, "No *sir*," and lifted my headset from the desk, bringing it down over my face.

I kept my eyes open and reminded myself of my mission: Save the other sixth graders, help Dad with Kandy Brainz, and make absolutely sure Mr. Underhill got busted by the Z.B.I.

Let's do this!

chapter 25

THE ANTS GO MARCHING one by one. Hurrah! Hurrah!

Straight into my brain.

I'm telling you, wearing that headset felt *weird*.

Ants and worms—that's the only way I know how to explain it.

At least that's how it felt in the beginning.

After the initial shock wore off, after I toggled past "*Z.O.M. Test 101: A Guide For 6th Graders,*" and finally logged into the encrypted DarkNite server—I didn't really feel anything at all.

Just numb.

Kinda warm, maybe? Like my brain was being microwaved. But then the game started up and I'm not going to lie—it was pretty cool.

DarkNite was, of course, *dark*. Like midnight when the moon goes behind a cloud. It felt so real. All I had to do was look a certain direction, and my character would begin walking that way. And my character was *me*.

All the way down to the blue Chucks. My DarkNite avatar was a carbon copy of Dashiell Storey: aged twelve years, dark brown hair, eighty-one pounds, four foot, six inches tall.

Creepy, but kinda cool.

How'd it know all that about me?

I didn't have time to find out before I saw something dart behind a dumpster in the distance. The best I could tell, I was in downtown Haven, right behind the Walmart. Everything looked exactly like it did in real life. Was this thing tapping into my memories?

Two black eyes peeked out from behind the dumpster.

My first instinct was to *run*!

Relax, dork. It's just a video game.

Okay, angry inner voice. You're right, *again*.

I moved my character forward, slowly. One step after another, and then I was standing right beside the dumpster. I took a deep breath. My heart—my *real* heart —pounded in my chest as I peered down into the darkness.

Awww. A wittle black *kitty*! It was so cute!

Bending down, I picked up the little fur ball. It purred and nestled its head against my chest.

This wasn't so bad. Not at all. In fact, I was starting to wonder why all the other kids were so addicted to DarkNite. It was basically like real life, just a little darker.

And then the cat got really heavy and meowed like crazy. It bolted from my arms, growing bigger and bigger as it scampered toward the dumpster again. Before the black kitten disappeared, I swear it stood up and started running on its hind legs.

I didn't move. I couldn't move. I didn't care if it was a video game or not—I was getting really scared.

"Dash?"

Okay, *now* I was *completely* freaked! That kitty just said my name!

"What are you doing playing DarkNite?"

The voice sounded so familiar.

I couldn't place it, though. Not until a girl stood up from behind the dumpster, laughing as she walked straight for me. The voice, the afro, it all came together and formed—

chapter 26

"Izzy!" I cried. "Wh-what are *you* doing here?"

Izzy just kept laughing as she took my hand. "I'm not really *here*, Dash. I'm just a product of your imagination."

I didn't know what to say.

"Everything in DarkNite comes from your memories," she explained. "You know, it's like when you're asleep but you know you're—"

"—*dreaming*," I said, finishing the sentence for her. "This is beyond weird."

Izzy giggled again. "You're so silly, Dash. Would you like for me to show you around?"

"I guess," I mumbled, still trying to make sense of this new world.

Izzy held my hand tight as we walked through the Walmart parking lot. It looked *exactly* like the one in real life. We continued on past Coventry Pond. Green slime still lined the banks, just how I remembered it. We weaved our way through Shadow Hills Cemetery. Every broken tombstone, every creepy shadow—they were all the same. Finally, we turned and headed for Haven Middle School.

"I don't get it," I said as we walked. "What's so cool about DarkNite?"

"You don't like it?" Izzy's voice sounded different, almost robotic.

"It's not that I don't like it," I muttered. "It's just that everything is the same."

Izzy started walking faster. "Wait till we get to school, Dash. Things are different at school."

I was beginning to worry about what I'd tell Agent Black. This whole ordeal had been pretty chill. Sure, a black cat morphed into Izzy Hendrix, but this *was* a video game. Right?

And then we were there, standing in front of my new school. Everything looked the same except the brick was darker and there were more shadows. Izzy pushed on the front doors and they swung open.

I guess that was different too. There weren't any locked doors in the DarkNite version of Haven Middle School.

Our sneakers squeaked in unison as we crept down the hall. We stopped in front of a familiar door. I could just make out the sign hanging above the room: *Underhill.*

A chill crawled across my shoulders and up my neck. I reminded myself it was just a game.

Izzy pushed the door open, and that's when things got *really* weird.

All the students turned and looked at me. Their headsets were pushed up on their heads, revealing their eyes.

"Dash! We're so glad you made it!" they shouted. The desks rattled as they stood, all together, and started moving across the classroom, coming our way.

"*Izzy,*" I whispered. "What the *what* is going on?"

My classmates were close now. Close enough I could see their eyes. They were dark. Totally black. They all started chanting, "*We want to be your friend, Dash. We want to be your…*"

"Izzy!" I screamed. "We've got to get out of here!"

She turned, slowly, to face me, and that's when I saw her eyes.

They were black and hollow, just like the rest of the kids.

"But, Dash," Izzy whispered. *"I want to be your friend, too."*

chapter 27

THERE WAS NO ESCAPE. I fully expected Mr. Underhill to emerge out from under his desk and start coming for my brainz...

But then a funny thing happened.

The kids stopped. They weren't coming for me. They weren't even chanting anymore.

I looked at Izzy. Her black, doll eyes were still super creepy, but there was something else... she looked like she was about to *cry*.

"You—you," Izzy stammered, "you don't want to be my friend?"

All the other kids said, "*Yeah?*" in unison, and it still sounded freaky, but I could tell they really meant it.

"No. Wait. I thought you guys were like coming to eat my brainz or something?"

"I'm sorry," Izzy said. "Did we scare you, Dash? We didn't mean to. We just really want to be your friend."

I scanned all the other kids' faces. Colt Taylor was standing in the front, closest to me, nodding his head.

"Yeah, Dash," he said. "I thought we were gonna be bros?"

And that's when I remembered—I was still in the video game. I was just playing DarkNite. This was *my* world. It was created from *my* memories, *my* imagination. No wonder all the kids came running, saying they wanted to be my friend. That's *exactly* what I wanted more than anything. *Friends.*

"Yeah," I said, feeling better by the second. "*Yeah.* We can all be friends."

They all bounced on their toes and clapped their hands. Colt stepped forward, draping his arm over my shoulder. "Well, Dash-man, what do you want to do now?"

I had a few ideas. Some crazy cool stuff that would get us into really big trouble if the teachers were around—

Teachers. Wait. Where were the teachers?

"Hey. *Izzy,*" I whispered, ducking out from under Colt's arm. "I, uh, I got to ask you something."

"Anything," Izzy said, smiling.

"Where's Underhill?"

"This is your world, Dash." Izzy's smile grew wider, stretching all the way up her cheeks, almost to her ears. "Mr. Underhill doesn't exist here."

Now I was the one smiling. "*Perfect*," I said, putting my arm over Colt Taylor's shoulder. I kinda had to get up on my tiptoes to do it. Colt was really tall.

"Listen up, fellow sixth graders," I announced. "Are you ready to have some fun?"

"Yeah!" they all shouted together.

"Then follow me!"

We ran down the halls. We chewed gum and stuck it under the teachers' chairs. We busted into Principal Manson's office and drew dragon wings on all her kitty pictures. We snuck into the cafeteria, chugged all the chocolate and strawberry milks, then dumped the white ones in the trash. We took the big rainbow-colored parachute out of the gym and onto the playground. We strung it up from the top of the basketball goal, like a giant pirate flag. Haven Middle School officially belonged to the kids!

And then, something unexpected happened: I got bored.

I plopped down on the bleachers beside the basketball court. The other students just kept standing there, spread out across the blacktop, waiting to see what fun idea I'd come up with next.

"I-I don't know what else to do," I said, speaking to the other kids. "I mean, we've basically done every crazy thing I could think of already."

They looked sad. A few of the girls' bottom lips quivered. Their eyes got red and watery.

Izzy stepped out of the crowd and sat down beside me. "You're not happy?"

"I just don't know what else to do. What's the point of this game anyway?"

"The point?" Izzy looked really confused. "What do you mean?"

"What's the point of DarkNite?"

"Oh," Izzy sighed. "I get it. You're just ready to move on to Level 2."

Level 2?

"Hey, guys?" Izzy shouted to the rest of the kids. "Dash is ready for Level 2!"

Their faces soured into frowns. Now the girls were really crying. I could hear them.

"Okay, Dash," Izzy said before I could figure out what was really happening. "Just remember, you asked for this."

Dark clouds rolled in across the sky. The whole playground dimmed, like a storm was coming. But it wasn't a storm. Standing in the back corner of the playground, I saw a man step out of the shadows.

A tall man, dressed from head to toe in black.

"Oh, hey," I said, standing up from the bleachers, pointing. "I know that guy. It's Agent Black."

"No," Izzy whispered. "It's not."

"*What?*"

"Dash, listen." Izzy's voice was serious now. "The game gets *real* in Level 2. It's not about having fun anymore. It's about *surviving.*"

I laughed in her face. This was *my* game, *my* world. I made the rules. "Come on. I think you'll like Agent Black. His first name's Frank. He's just a big teddy bear."

I started to push my way through the crowd of frozen kids, but Izzy grabbed hold of my arm.

"Hey, knock it off," I said, turning, and what I saw made my blood run cold.

Izzy's big black eyes were wide open. She looked terrified.

And then I felt a cold hand on my shoulder. I didn't have to turn. I could see the man's reflection in Izzy's black eyes.

"He—he's standing right behind you." Izzy's lips barely moved as she spoke. "Dash, promise you'll come for me. Promise you won't forget."

I didn't have a clue what she was talking about.

I didn't have time to find out.

The man's arm came over my shoulder and grabbed Izzy by her flowery dress. He lifted her, like she didn't weigh anything, up and over my head.

When I turned, the man was standing so close I could see his face. Shadows swirled across his cheeks, drifting in and out of his eyes.

This guy was *not* Special Agent Frank Black. This freak-a-zoid—this *monster*—was *The Man In Black*.

chapter 28

"*Promise!*" Izzy screamed, squirming in the dark man's grip. "You have to come for me, Dash! *Promise* you won't forget!"

My mouth opened. I wanted to tell her everything would be okay, but before I could the Man In Black laughed. It sounded like a thousand pigs squealing, and then he disappeared, taking Izzy with him. A cloud of black smoke was all that remained.

My fingertips tingled. My feet felt cold and numb. I

turned, slowly, back to the bleachers. The kids were all just standing there, staring at me with their black doll eyes.

"What just happened?" I whispered.

Their faces were frozen, like the game had glitched or something. And then Colt stepped forward.

"You lost her, Dash. You let The Man In Black take her away."

"But..." I felt a lump rise in my throat. I swallowed it down. "How do we get her back?"

"We?" Colt said. "I'm sorry, Dash, but *we* can't help you."

"*Wait*," I snapped. "You guys were supposed to be my *friends*, and now I need your help."

"I'm sorry," Colt said. "I really am, but this is your game. It's all a part of your imagination."

"So you mean... *I'm* the reason Izzy was taken away?"

Colt nodded in slo-mo.

"But... I would've never wanted something bad to happen to Izzy."

Colt turned to the rest of the students and snapped his fingers. They still had their headsets resting on top of their heads. They pushed them down over their eyes. The beeping sound I'd heard on my first day at Haven echoed out across the playground. The students lined up, single file, and started marching back toward the school.

"Wait!" I shouted, grabbing Colt's arm before he got in line with the others. "What can I do? How do I get her back?"

Colt jerked away so fast, so hard, I tripped just trying to keep my hold on him. My palms scraped against the pavement as I fell.

"You want her back?" Colt said, standing over me. "Then you've got to play the game."

And then he was gone, already marching in line with the others.

Bright red blood bubbled up on my palms. It hurt. It felt *so* real. What was Colt talking about? I thought I *was* playing the game?

A scream exploded out across the playground. A high-pitched, bone-chilling scream.

The Man In Black stood on the far side of the playground, back close to the road. He still had Izzy in his arms, but she looked different somehow.

"Hey!" I shouted. "Give her back."

I started to run. The closer I got, the more I saw of Izzy. It wasn't pretty. Black shadows were spilling out of her doll eyes, covering her cheeks, her nose, creeping their way up her forehead. It was like she was being erased.

"You hear me!" I screamed. "You give her—"

Before I could get the rest of the sentence out, my whole world flipped upside down. An explosion of light. Everything so bright I couldn't see anything for a few seconds, like a bomb had gone off.

I blinked, hoping Izzy was still up there, waiting for me, but when my world came back into focus, I was staring straight into Mr. Underhill's yellow eyes.

"Dash?" he said, squatting down in front of my desk, blowing his nasty brain breath right in my face. "You must have really been studying hard for the Z.O.M. Test. You were screaming like crazy."

"I–I—" There were no words for what I'd just experienced. "I'm sorry. I think I fell asleep. I think I was having a bad dream."

"A nightmare?" Mr. Underhill laughed. "That's what you think?"

Maybe he knew I was playing DarkNite. I was too freaked to find out. My headset was pushed up in my hair. I reached for it and started to pull it down.

"What are you doing?"

"I, uh, I need to keep studying for the test."

Mr. Underhill laughed again as he pointed to the

clock. I squinted, reading the numbers, and then I realized the classroom was completely empty. Where were all the other kids?

"School's over, Dash," Mr. Underhill said. "It's time for you to go home."

chapter 29

WHEN THE MYSTERY Machine pulled up in the school parking lot, I was still trying to shake my headset hangover. It felt like when Mom comes into my room first thing in the morning, turns on all the lights, throws back the covers, and I still don't want to get out of bed.

But worse.

The whole drive home I didn't say a single word. Mom kept trying to get me to talk, asking the same old questions: *How was school today? Do you have any homework?* Maybe I should've answered her. Maybe I would've felt better if I talked to Mom, but I couldn't. I'd read too many books. I'd seen too many scary movies. Kids *never* talked to their parents in those stories. They just kept going, and by the end, they always figured out a way to beat the bad guy. This was something I had to do on my own.

I watched Haven drift past through the window, trying to make sense of what had happened. The streets, the parking lot, even slimy old Coventry Pond—everything looked different now. I couldn't tell what was fake and what was real.

The Mystery Machine turned onto our street, and I started to wonder when, exactly, I'd be able to give my report to Agent Black. Maybe if I told him tonight, I wouldn't have to wear the headset anymore.

But what about—

Izzy.

It was like she'd just appeared out of nowhere, standing in the front yard of her big, creepy house. She didn't wave as the Mystery Machine drove by. She didn't even smile. She just stood there, staring at me. And her eyes...

They were *huge* and *black*, just like they'd been in DarkNite.

"Stop the car!" I cried. "Mom, please!"

The brakes hissed.

"*Dash,*" Mom snapped. "What's gotten into you?"

"I'm fine, Mom. Everything's fine," I lied, my hand already reaching for the van's side door. "I just need to go talk to Izzy."

"*Izzy?*" Mom spun around in the front seat. "Dash, I'm worried about *you*."

"I'll be home before supper," I said, out of the van now, already sliding the door shut. "I promise."

And then I was running across the street, through the dead, yellow grass in Izzy's front yard. Her house was even creepier up close. There wasn't a light on anywhere. It definitely looked haunted.

Izzy sat on the front porch steps, chin resting on her knees.

"Hey," I said as my feet thudded to a stop. "Are you okay?"

She just kept sitting there. She didn't look up.

"Why weren't you at school today?"

"Oh, Dash," she whispered. "There's so much you don't know."

"Are you sick? Is this like some sort of *girl* problem?"

Izzy looked straight at me. "You were supposed to save them."

"The sixth graders?" I sat down beside her on the steps. "I'm working on it, Izzy. There's just some stuff I can't tell you right now."

She pulled her knees in close to her chest. "Books,

Dash. That's what you're supposed to be working on. Getting the other kids to read. That's the only way."

I almost laughed. I wanted so bad to tell her about my classified mission, about Agent Black, and how I was working for the Z.B.I. Honestly, books were about the farthest thing from my mind.

"Izzy, listen—" I started, but then she cut me off.

"No, Dash. *You* listen."

She turned to face me, and that's when I saw her eyes again. They were still big and black, like two huge dilated pupils.

"You were supposed to save *me*," she whispered.

An image flashed across my brain: The Man In Black dragging Izzy away.

"But instead," her voice was quiet now, "you did the one thing I told you never to do."

Wait. What? Izzy wasn't at school today. How did she know?

"You played DarkNite." Her head fell into her hands and her shoulders started jerking up and down.

"Izzy, please. Let me explain." I took a deep breath, ready to tell my only friend everything if that's what it took to make her believe me. "I'm on this super-secret mission. I went undercover today because—"

The purr of a car engine cut my words short. I

looked up. A long black sedan crept slowly down the road. It came to a stop right in front of my house.

"All because of *him*," Izzy said and pointed toward the black car.

My stomach flipped, like when Dad drives The Brain-Mobile too fast over a hill.

"You—you know about Agent Black?" I could barely get the words out.

"Yes. I know about him," Izzy said. "I know *everything*."

The way she said that last line—I'm not gonna lie—it was kinda freaky.

"What do you know?" I said, but Izzy had her face buried in her hands again, shoulders jerking up and down.

"It's too late now, Dash," Izzy whimpered.

"What does that even mean?"

Tears drizzled out around Izzy's fingers, cutting lines down her cheek.

"Izzy," I pleaded. "Why are you so upset?"

All at once, her head jerked back from her hands. Her face was an awful mixture of anger and pain. "I'm upset," she snarled, wiping her nose with the back of her hand, "because of you, Dash Storey."

"Me?"

"Yes, *you*," Izzy snapped, standing up from the stairs, turning for her creepy house's front door.

"Wait," I said, standing now too. "Where are you going?"

A car door slammed shut behind me. It was loud enough I had to turn and look.

Agent Black was walking across my front lawn. When he came to the door, he knocked, just like he'd done the day before, and then he did something really weird.

He turned and looked straight at me.

From across the street, his face looked all freaky again. The shadows were back, or maybe I was just imagining things. Maybe I was still feeling the effects of my headset hangover. The front door opened, and Mom welcomed the Special Agent inside.

Something still didn't feel right, though. Izzy was *way* too upset about me playing a stupid video game. I turned back to her, hoping maybe she was feeling better now and ready to talk, but the porch was empty.

"Izzy?" I whispered.

The front door cracked open, just barely. I took a step toward it, but a voice stopped me dead in my tracks.

"Go away."

Two eyes appeared behind the door.

"*Izzy?*"

"Leave me alone, Dash Storey," the voice croaked. The two eyes glowed hot in the darkness. "I don't ever want to see you again."

The door slammed shut in my face. I was so confused. Izzy was seriously ticked, but why?

"*Dash?*"

A different voice now, coming from behind me. I turned and saw Mom standing out in our front yard. "Dash, it's time to come home." Mom shouted. "*Dash!* I'm not telling you again!"

"I'm coming," I moaned and turned away.

Izzy's house stood dead silent behind me.

chapter 30

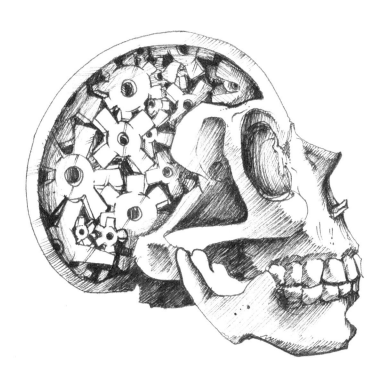

WALKING up the front porch steps and into my house, I couldn't get Izzy's final words out of my mind:

"I don't ever want to see you again!"

I was so busy trying to figure out why she'd gone so crazy on me, I didn't even notice Agent Black sitting in the La-Z-Boy recliner. I didn't notice the brown folder in his hand, or how Mom and Dad were standing over near the mantle, huddled together like they were scared.

Then I noticed everything, all at once, and none of it made sense.

My sneakers slid to a stop on the hardwood floors. The fridge's ice maker clicked on and growled, but still, the grownups stayed silent.

"Agent Black, my man," I said, hoping maybe I could lighten the mood. "You're looking really good today. All that black goes great with your skin tone."

Dad stepped forward, glancing back over his shoulder at Mom.

"*Agent Black?*" Dad said. "Where do you come up with this stuff, Dash?"

So *that's* what this was about. My parents were snooping on me last night. They must have heard about my undercover work for the Z.B.I. and now they were, what, *jealous?*

"Easy, Dad," I said, staring at the Special Agent sitting in my living room. "You're asking about *classified* information. Do you even know what that means?"

Dad's face got all red. His mouth opened, but I cut him off.

"Tell him, Agent Black," I said, walking across the living room toward the recliner. "Tell him what you told me last night."

The Special Agent finally looked away from the window, leveling his dark eyes out on mine. "Please,

Dash..." His voice was soft, not at all like I remembered. "Stop calling me that."

I laughed right in his face. "They're on to us. So just tell them about my super-secret mission, how I'm working for the Z.B.I. You know, Zom-Corp and the headsets. You might as well tell them everything now."

Sunlight poured in through the blinds, casting sideways rays across Agent Black's pale face. I kept looking at him, waiting for him to nod, or at least say *something*. There was only silence. Complete and utter silence.

"Come on," I snapped. "You could at least tell them about Underhill."

"Your new teacher?" Mom whispered across the room.

I turned because her voice sounded so weak. Her eyes were red, her cheeks wet. She was *crying*, just like Izzy had been. What the heck was going on?

"Yeah, Mom. Mr. Underhill," I said. "My new teacher—he's a brain-munchin' zombie."

Mom's quiet tears were replaced with a gut-wrenching moan. She pushed her face into Dad's shoulder. He ran a hand through her hair and looked at me.

"I don't get it," I mumbled. "What'd I do?"

"What'd you do?" Dad barked. "You were suspended from school yesterday, Dash. You haven't been studying for the Zone One Marker Test. *And* you just told us you think your teacher is a *zombie!*"

His voice echoed across the hardwood floor.

"Mr. Underhill *is* a zombie," I hissed. I couldn't help it. It was the truth, and if I didn't say something now, my freak-a-zoid teacher was going to have a full-on brain buffet come Friday.

"Stop it, Dash." Mom said, her face twisted and angry. "You have to stop this lying."

"Lying!" I shouted so loud my throat hurt. "It's the *truth*, Mom, and if you don't believe me just ask Izzy Hendrix!"

Tears poured from Mom's eyes again. Her mouth kept moving, gulping like a fish out of water, but she couldn't get anything out.

And then Agent Black stood up from the recliner. I'd forgotten how tall he was. His head almost touched the fan hanging down from the middle of the ceiling.

"Dashiell," Agent Black said, a calm, quiet tone despite the chaos. "We already talked about Izzy."

My brain buzzed, trying to remember the conversation with Agent Black from the night before. I knew for a fact I hadn't said anything to him about Izzy Hendrix. Not a single word.

"You promised," he said, stepping forward. "You promised me that you would forget her."

Forget? I didn't say that word last night, did I?

I just remembered playing DarkNite. The way Izzy had screamed when The Man In Black—the one in the video game—took her away. *"Promise you won't forget, Dash!"* My brain glitched, trying to make sense of everything.

"Forget her?" I managed, choking back tears of my own. "Why do you want me to forget Izzy Hendrix?"

Agent Black's chest rose and fell. He squatted down, looking me straight in the eyes.

"You must forget her, Dash," he said, "because she isn't *real*."

chapter 31

SOMETIMES, when I get in really big trouble—like that time I drew my very own Batman comic on the front of Dad's latest Kandy Brainz report—I start laughing. Like a wicked supervillain cackle. I can't help it.

Which was exactly what I did when Agent Black told me Izzy didn't exist.

"You–you—" I caught myself between belly laughs and tried to breathe. "You've *got* to be kidding me. Come on, Agent Black. I never took you for such a kidder."

He was still kneeling in front of me. "My name," he said, eyes narrowing as he nodded very seriously, "is Dr. Franklin Blackwell. I'm a child psychologist. I was hired by your parents to come here and help you with this transition."

I wasn't laughing anymore. If I had thought my brain was glitching before, it was like totally frozen now. My whole world stopped spinning as Agent Black—I mean, wait—*Dr. Franklin Blackwell* continued his speech:

"Your parents, Dashiell, they were worried about you, so they called me to come help. They wanted me to see how you were adjusting to your new school. You know, follow you around."

So *that's* why this guy had been following me? My parents *hired* him?

"I went over all of this last night, but you wouldn't listen. You just kept calling me 'Agent Black,' and carrying on about the Z.B.I." Dr. Blackwell paused, like he was letting it all sink in. "It's a common coping mechanism I see with kids your age, coming up with stories that are easier than the truth. You seem to have taken the move to Haven especially hard."

My teeth clamped down on my bottom lip. I started chewing.

"And judging by these write ups," Dr. Blackwell

said, flipping over the brown folder in his hands, "you're having some serious trouble at school."

"Wh-where'd you get that?"

"I've been working very closely with Principal Manson," Dr. Blackwell explained.

I remembered seeing him in her office the day Colt and I got in trouble.

"Principal Manson is worried too," Dr. Blackwell added, still thumbing through the folder. "She told me about how you opened up to her yesterday. Told her about how much stress you felt because of your family's latest move."

"I should've known better than to trust that cat-loving principal."

"*Dash*," Mom croaked. "Are you even listening?"

Yeah, I'd heard every word this goober was telling me, but I didn't believe him. No way. As far as I knew, this was all some big set up, some sort of test. I lifted my chin at Mom and turned back to my "*psychologist*."

"It says here in the folder," Dr. Blackwell's index finger tapped loudly against the papers, "that on Monday you slept for the entire day."

"Now wait a second," I tried, but Blackwell talked over me.

"Straight through lunch, up until the school bell rang," he said. "And then, yesterday—as we all know—

you were suspended. I picked up today's report from your teacher on my way over, and Dashiell, I'm afraid his write up is worst of all."

I shook my head, taking one step back, then another. I needed to get out of there. I needed to talk to someone who would listen.

It was like Dad could read my mind or something. He let go of Mom and hurried across the room, blocking any chance I had of making a run for the door.

"Tell us, Doc," Dad said. "What'd Dash do at school today?"

Dr. Blackwell sighed, like he didn't really want to say it, but then he did. "Dash logged eight straight hours on a video game called DarkNite."

"Eight hours!" Mom screeched. "You didn't even eat lunch?"

I ignored her, pointing at Blackwell now. "I did what *you* told me to do," I snapped. "That big talk we had last night? I was just following your 'classified' orders."

Dr. Blackwell shook his head. "I said nothing of the sort, Dashiell. You're making up stories again, stories that fit your world. I urged you to get serious about the Zone One Marker Test. That exam is extremely important for your future. But you just kept talking about the Z.B.I. and your top-secret mission."

"You're lying!" I shouted and turned for the door.

Dad hunkered down like he was back on a football field, ready to make the tackle. I pointed at him. "And you!" I shouted. "You guys think *I'm* lying, but I'm not, and I can prove it."

I started toward Dad. He might've been big and strong, but I was quick. Maybe I could juke him out and get through the door.

"Wait!" Mom cried.

There was so much pain in her voice, I had to stop.

"There's nothing left to prove," she whispered. "After everything Dr. Blackwell just said, what else is there to explain?"

"I have a friend, a real friend," I said and didn't look at Mom. I didn't want to see the pain in her eyes. "Her name is Izzy Hendrix."

Dad chuckled and raised both hands. "Come on, Dash. I know I told you to make friends at school, but this—"

Before he could say anything else, I charged past him, like a running back slicing through the line of scrimmage. He was so busy laughing, looking from Mom to Dr. Blackwell in disbelief, he never saw me coming. I slipped past him and out the door.

My blue Chucks flew across the yard, into the street, and before I knew it, I was standing on the front porch of

Izzy's creepy old house. I could hear my parents and Dr. Blackwell's footsteps behind me. There was no time for knocking, no time for anything other than finding Izzy Hendrix and proving them all wrong.

I took a deep breath and opened the door.

chapter 32

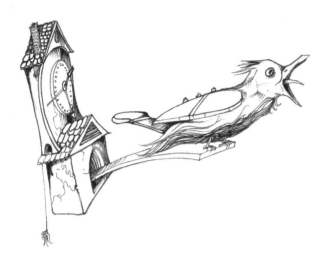

"Izzy?"

Imagine the absolute *freakiest* place you've ever seen in a scary movie and multiply it by ten.

"*Izzy.*"

The huge staircase in the foyer was covered in cobwebs. An antique cuckoo clock hung from a wall in the corner. The crazy-eyed bird stood frozen with its beak open, like it was screaming, *Get out! Get out!* There wasn't another piece of furniture in the rest of the house.

"*IZZY!*" I screamed her name this time, as loud as I could, and then I waited.

My own voice was all I heard, echoing back down that creepy staircase.

"Dashiell?"

I turned immediately, not even wondering why Izzy had just called me "Dashiell." Nobody called me my full name, except—

"Oh," I groaned. "It's you."

Dr. Blackwell (formerly known as Agent Black) was standing in the doorway.

"Well," he said. "Did you find her?"

I thought about calling for Izzy again, but I remembered how peeved she'd been at me earlier. She *was* here. I knew it. She was probably just hiding.

"I'd like to show you something," Dr. Blackwell said, turning sideways in the door and lifting his hand.

I could see his face now, the pale skin with the dark stubble sprouting up across his chin.

"Come on." His voice was soft, like he was calling a lost puppy. "This won't take long."

"Whatever."

As we walked through the door, across the porch, and back on to the sidewalk, I kept waiting to see Mom and Dad. But the street was empty. A few kids were bouncing a basketball in a driveway up the road. That was it.

"Where are my parents?" I asked.

Dr. Blackwell kept his head down and his hands jammed in his pockets, walking out a good ways ahead of me.

"*Hey*," I snapped. "I asked you a question."

"They're waiting for us, Dashiell. You'll see them soon enough."

My chest went tight.

"Wh-where are we going?"

The doctor walked on, taking long strides, and then we were standing on the edge of Coventry Pond. The green water glowed in the evening light. We made our way around the bank as the sun dipped down behind the crumbling roof of Izzy's house.

When we came to Shadow Hills Cemetery, the light was almost gone. The tombstones, the fresh mounds of dirt, everything was covered in the dark shadows of the dying day.

Even Mom and Dad.

I saw them up ahead of us, standing over a grave like they were at a funeral.

My feet went all tingly, and then a light bulb flashed above my head.

"*Hey*," I shouted, reaching up and tugging on Dr. Blackwell's black coat. "Hey, Doc, listen. I've got an idea!"

He walked faster, dragging me through the graveyard.

"You hear me?" My feet slid across the dead grass. "I can *prove* I'm not lying. Just let me show them the—"

And then he stopped. All at once. I was tugging so hard, I lost my balance and fell face first in front of my parents. I squirmed around in the dirt, trying to right myself. When I looked up, Mom, Dad, and Dr. Blackwell were all just standing there, looking down on me.

"Dash," Mom said, stepping forward a little. "We don't know what's been going on with you. We don't know why you won't snap out of it, but we're here for you. I want you to know that."

I was down on all fours. Mom's voice sounded far away.

"Turn around, son." Dad said, moving up beside Mom. "Turn around and read us the name on that tombstone."

"You already *know!*" I cried, thinking maybe they'd brought me here to show me what I was going to show them. I turned my head and my eyes followed. I fully expected to see *Lonnie Underhill* etched across the crumbling stone, but I was wrong, *dead* wrong.

"Read it, Dashiell."

I was so shocked by the name I saw, I could barely hear Dr. Blackwell's voice.

"Read the name aloud," he said. "It will help make this a reality."

The empty haunted house. The way she wasn't at school. How she seemed to just disappear and reappear whenever she wanted—all those details swirled around in my brain and exploded as I spoke the name etched across that tombstone:

"Isabelle Hendrix."

THURSDAY

chapter 33

It took me all of Wednesday night and most of Thursday to come to terms with the fact that Izzy was dead. The way Dr. Blackwell explained it—she'd been dead for a really long time.

Isabelle "Izzy" Hendrix drowned in Coventry Pond back around 1970. The same year Jimi Hendrix died. Dr. Blackwell said I'd dreamed her up. He said it was actually quite normal for kids my age to have an "imaginary" friend, but he'd never encountered such an extreme case. I'd completely made up all that stuff about the Z.B.I. and my top-secret mission, not to mention Izzy.

Dad tried to blame my overactive imagination on the scary movies I liked so much and all those freaky books I read. Mom said maybe her infatuation with Jimi Hendrix had something to do with it, too. Maybe she'd listened to "Voodoo Chile" in the Mystery Machine one too many times.

Walking back from the cemetery that night felt a lot like taking the headset off. Like coming out of a dream. The real world was dull and gray without Izzy Hendrix around.

Dr. Blackwell never said anything about Mr. Underhill. There was no talk of the headsets or zombies. He didn't even prescribe me any medication. He just told me to write. He said I should start a journal. That way I could keep my thoughts in order. Honestly, the last thing I wanted to do was start a stupid diary.

In the end, Mom and Dad still grounded me. Or wait, I guess "grounded" wasn't really the right word. They made a "deal" with me, instead.

"So, here's the deal," Dad said late Wednesday night, looking down on me in the living room. "You ace that Z.O.M. Test, Dash-man, and then we'll talk about giving you your stuff back."

I was still feeling kinda woozy, kinda shocked, but that snapped me out of it.

"Stuff?" I stammered. "What *stuff*?"

"Your books. Those creepy movies you like so much."

Dad said it so matter-of-fact, I almost couldn't believe it. Those were the only things I had. Period. No friends. No sports. That *stuff* was my whole world.

"Don't forget the other part, honey," Mom added.

Dad cleared his throat. "If we get any bad reports, a single write up saying you logged on to that video game, then there will be no trick-or-treating Friday."

"Big deal," I mumbled, staring straight back at Mom and Dad, feeling empty on the inside. "Halloween's for little kids, anyway."

I don't know if I really meant it—I didn't know what to believe anymore—but it didn't matter. I stomped up the stairs, crawled into bed, and fell into a deep sleep.

The next morning was a blur. A whole pointless school day came and went, and I did just like they told me. I was a good boy. I studied hard for the Z.O.M. Test. If you can even call it studying. It was more like downloading. The headset streamed all this pointless information into my brain: the Quadratic Equation, the Pythagorean Theorem, and the Scientific Method. Hypotheses and all that junk. It seemed like the whole test was just Math and Science. My two worst subjects.

I was so bored my brain felt like scrambled eggs. I

thought about logging on to DarkNite. Maybe Izzy would be there. Maybe this time I could save her from The Man In Black. Maybe she'd come back to life and things would go back to normal. But I didn't. I was too scared. And I wanted my books and my movies back. *Bad.* Deep down, I guess I really wanted to get out of the house on Halloween, too. I didn't care about the candy. Not really. I just wanted freedom.

And then it was Thursday night.

The day before the Z.O.M Test.

Halloween Eve.

I crawled into bed and stared at the ceiling, wishing I had a book to read or a movie to watch. Jawz kept swimming up to the edge of his glass bowl and staring out at the empty place where my big, beautiful flat-screen TV had been.

All that remained of my forty-two-inch Samsung were black cords, spiraling out from the wall like snakes. Every one of my books were gone too. The shelves bare. Jawz floated back down to the bottom of his bowl. He looked lost, maybe even a little sad.

I stared at the ceiling. I couldn't sleep. Not without a book in my hands. Not without a movie going in the background.

I closed my eyes, trying to go over some of the junk I

had learned at school earlier: *The Scientific Method is a seven-step process used to solve—*

And that's when I heard it. Something scratching at my window.

I tried to reason the sound away using the Scientific Method.

Observation: *Something just scraped against my window.*

Hypothesis: *It's just the wind.*

But then it happened again. *Screeech.* Louder this time.

I had my Batman bed sheets up under my chin, too scared to move. Then I remembered everything Dr. Blackwell had said, how I have an "overactive" imagination. How I see things that aren't real.

I threw the sheets back, swung my legs out of the bed, and stepped toward the window. When I got there, I could hear the wind whipping outside. I watched as a skinny tree limb scraped the glass.

Hypothesis proved.

Despite having just correctly used the Scientific Method, I felt kinda dumb. I just stood there, staring out the window. The sky was dark and swirling, like maybe a storm was blowing in. I looked past the rustling tree limbs to the creepy old house on the corner. I kept staring at it, hoping, maybe, a blue light would appear in the tiny window on the second floor.

Tip-toeing my way back to bed, I suddenly felt really sleepy.

Get some rest, kid. You're gonna need it for that test tomorrow.

"Whoa," I whispered. "Angry inner voice isn't so angry anymore?"

I pulled the covers back and waited for a response. So yeah, I'd stopped seeing dead people, but now I was seriously talking to myself. I kept waiting. I didn't have anything else to do, and that's when I heard my name.

"Dash?"

It could've just been the wind again, whistling up the drainpipe outside my window.

"Dash, uh, why are you ignoring me?"

Okay. Screw the Scientific Method. That wasn't the wind.

A huge bolt of lightning flashed outside my window, followed immediately by a thunderous *boom*. The house rattled, the lights flickered—once, twice—and then everything went black.

chapter 34

I HAD the bed sheets all the way up over my head. I was *not* imagining this. The lights were definitely off, and someone—or some*thing*—kept saying my name.

"Daaa*sh*."

"You're not real," I whispered, my breath hot beneath the covers. "You're *not* real."

"Who says?" the voice answered.

I *knew* that voice. I peeked out from under the sheets, and that's when I saw her.

"*Izzy?*"

"In the flesh," she said, floating down by the foot of

my bed, floating like a ghost floats, all blue and transparent and stuff.

"Okay, so not *in the flesh*," she giggled. "But you get it."

"Izzy!"

I was out of bed and running for my best friend, planning to wrap my arms around her, give her the biggest, dorkiest hug *ever*, but my arms just went right through her.

She floated back away from me, laughing.

"You–you—" I stammered. "You're a ghost?"

Izzy rolled her ghost eyes. They spun all the way up into her skull. Her dark black pupils appeared again up from the bottom, like some sort of eyeball backflip. *Creepy*.

"I'm whatever you want me to be, Dash."

"But you're dead," I whispered. "Dr. Blackwell, he showed me your grave. Told me about how you drowned in—"

"—Coventry Pond?" Izzy said, still smiling. "Yeah, stay away from slimy green water. *Especially*, if you don't know how to swim."

I was just standing there, my bare feet cold on the hardwood floors. And Izzy was *floating*. All the lights were out. It was raining hard now. The wind rushed against my window as more lightning flashed and thunder rolled. Izzy was the only light in my dark room, glowing like a dim blue bulb. It was too much. I blinked and hoped when my eyes opened again she'd be gone.

"Uh, Dash?" Izzy snapped. "What are you doing?"

"You're not real," I said, blinking again. "You *can't* be real."

She floated down to my bed and sat right on Batman's face. I could still see Batman's pointy ears, because, well, Izzy was transparent.

"Like I said, I'm whatever you want me to be."

She patted the place on the bed beside her. The sheets didn't move, didn't wrinkle, nothing.

"Come on, dork. Sit down."

I shook my head. This was too much.

"Didn't you think it was weird the way I dressed and stuff?" Izzy folded her hands in her lap. She was still wearing that flowery dress. The same one she *always* wore. That should've been my first clue. What kid wears the same clothes every single day?

"The flower-power sun dress? The straight-outta-the-70s afro?" Izzy grinned and stuck her thumb in her mouth. Her cheeks ballooned out, like she was blowing really hard, and then that glorious afro started to grow. Bigger and bigger, like a huge dark cloud.

"*Epic.*"

"I know, right?" Izzy popped her thumb out of her mouth and her afro shrunk back down.

Izzy being a ghost was way cooler than I expected, but then I remembered the last time I'd seen her. How she'd slammed the door in my face. The mean words she'd said.

"I, uh, I thought you were mad at me or something?"

Izzy floated off the bed and came around in front of me. "I *was* mad at you, Dash. You did the one thing I told you never to do."

"I played DarkNite."

"Duh. And I guess I'm still kinda mad, but we don't have much time."

"Time?"

"The Z.O.M. Test is tomorrow. You still have to stop Mr. Underhill."

I stood and started shaking my head. "Please," I mumbled. "Just stop, Izzy. I'm already super confused."

"But the other kids," Izzy snapped. "You're their only hope."

Backing away from her, I rammed my butt into the bedroom door. "No, Izzy. You're not even real."

"Who gets to decide what's real and what's not?" Izzy snapped, hovering closer and closer to me. "Your parents? Some creepy child psychologist? Mr. *Underhill?* Nuh-uh. No way!"

Izzy's voice kept getting louder and louder. I slipped my hand behind my back and slid my fingers around the doorknob.

"You're the only one that can save them, Dash!" Izzy's voice sounded like the wind whistling through the trees.

"No!" I shouted, turning the doorknob, and then a different voice called out from the first floor.

"Dash? Everything okay up there?"

It was Mom! The last thing I needed was for my parents to come barging into the room and find Izzy. Or worse, what if they'd already heard me talking to myself? I'd *never* get my books back.

"Uh..." I couldn't think of what to say.

And then I heard footsteps coming up the stairs.

chapter 35

I KEPT my back pressed to the door. There was *no way* I was letting Mom in here. Not with the ghost of Izzy Hendrix floating around.

The footsteps came to a stop at the top of the stairs.

"Dash?" Mom whispered. "Is everything all right?"

"Uh–uh..."

"I thought I heard you talking? Open the door, Dash."

I still couldn't think of what to say.

"Tell her you had a bad dream," Izzy whispered.

Her voice sounded like it came from inside my head. Everything glowed blue and my face felt warm. My eyes darted back around my dark room, but I didn't see Izzy anywhere.

"*Dash?*" Mom said, louder this time.

"Hurry up, dork," Izzy snapped. "Tell her it was just a nightmare."

"I, uh—" I mumbled. "It was just a bad dream, Mom. Everything's fine."

"You're sure? Do I need to come tuck you in?"

"*Tuck you in?*" Izzy snorted. "You really are a *dork*."

There was something about the way Izzy just called me "dork," that sounded super familiar. I was so busy trying to figure out what it was, I didn't notice the doorknob turning in my hand.

"No, Mom! Wait!" I blurted, slamming against the door with all my strength. "I'm not wearing any pants!"

The door smacked shut and echoed through the house. I had no idea where that last line had come from. I could hear Mom breathing through the crack in the door.

"Okay, Dash," she said, softly. "The power is out. Big

thunderstorm blew up about a half hour ago. Try to get some rest."

"Yeah, Mom."

"And put some pants on. Geez."

"Right," I managed. "Pants. Got it."

Her footsteps clacked back down the stairs. I waited until I couldn't hear them anymore, then pressed my back against the door and slid down. My room was completely black. I didn't see Izzy anywhere.

"Alright," I said. "She's gone. You can come out now."

A few seconds passed, and then I heard: "I'm right here. Don't you see me?"

My room was so dark. I couldn't see anything.

"Wait. Of course you can't see me," Izzy said. "But can you at least *feel* me?"

That's when I noticed the blue glow and that warm fuzzy feeling again. It was like I was wrapped in a thick wool blanket.

"I'm inside of you, dork." Izzy's voice echoed like an electric guitar with a super long delay. "Right where I've been all along."

There it was again. That familiar word. "Dork." Suddenly, everything made sense.

"You're my angry inner voice?" I said, watching as

the blue glow poured out of me, and Izzy returned to ghost form right before my very eyes.

"I wouldn't say *angry*," she said and smiled. "I'm more like your voice of reason. You dreamed me up when you moved to Haven. Just like Dr. Blackwell explained. You needed a friend, Dash. So you imagined one."

"But that grave in Shadow Hills?" I said. "It's really yours?"

"Sure, I guess. I mean, there's some dead girl named Isabelle Hendrix buried under there. You probably just saw her name and thought it was cool."

My head hurt. I was so tired. If I was going to have any chance at all of passing the Z.O.M. Test tomorrow, I needed to sleep.

"Izzy," I said, standing, already headed for my bed. "This is cool and all, but listen, I really need to get some rest."

"*Rest!* What are you talking about?" she barked, hovering down in front of me like she could actually block my path. I walked right through her.

"Dash," she moaned, floating over me as I crawled back into bed. "What about the other kids? What about *Underhill!*"

"You said it yourself, Izzy. Everything has just been a product of my crazy imagination. Besides," I said, pointing over to my empty bookshelves, "Dad took all my books, all my movies, he even took my TV."

"Your books," Izzy whispered. "They're *gone?*"

"All of them. Now will you please let me get some rest?"

I rolled over, snuggling up close to my pillow, and then my Batman sheets went flying through the air. They hit the far wall with a soft thump.

"Izzy," I groaned, rolling out of bed. "What's your deal?"

She floated over toward the crumpled sheets and lifted them in the air.

"My deal," she said, "is that you still have work to do. You have to save the other sixth graders."

"I already told you I don't have any of my books. Even if I *did* have them, none of the other kids at Haven would read them. Their brainz are mush. They've spent *way* too much time playing DarkNite."

Izzy dropped the sheets and floated back down toward me. She kept getting closer and closer, and then she disappeared.

"Not fair," I snapped. "You're back inside my head again."

"Just listen, dork." Izzy's voice rattled around my skull. It kinda tickled. "You're right about two things: First, the Haven kids' brainz *are* mush. They're rotten, just like the zombies want them. Second, there's no chance they'll read any of those old weird books you like so much."

"I don't get it," I said, standing in my dark, silent room. "If you already know they're not going to read any of those books, then what's the point?"

I could feel Izzy laughing inside my head. She slid out of my nose in a long blue cloud, smiling from ghost ear to ghost ear.

"You're going to write a book for them," Izzy said. "One that's even cooler than DarkNite."

chapter 36

I REMEMBERED Dr. Blackwell urging me to start a diary. How he'd said it would help keep my thoughts in order. What Izzy was asking me to do was different. Way different. I'd scribbled out a few stories in my composition notebooks before, but I'd never written a *book!*

"This is crazy," I said. "*You're* crazy."

"If I'm crazy, then that means you're crazy too."

Good point, I thought, and then Izzy started laughing.

"I'm inside your head, dork. I can hear your thoughts."

I tried not to think about anything, but my brain darted back and forth, going over the gazillion reasons why I couldn't write a book.

"Ugh," Izzy groaned. "I'm listening to every reason you're thinking right now... Yes, the power is still out. We'll have to think of a way around that one. And, no, you've never written a book before, but listen, Dash, I can help."

I stood there, still trying not to think anything, and waited for Izzy to tell me her big plan.

"Just like I helped you when your mom was about to barge in here," she said. "Remember? I came up with the idea about having the bad dream."

"Yeah," I said and walked over to my desk. Jawz swam a fast circle, like he was happy to see me. "But I came up with the part about not being dressed."

"That's right!" Izzy screeched. "See! We make an *amazing* team!"

I groaned and sat down at my desk, looking up at all my empty bookshelves.

"So the stuff about Mr. Underhill, about him being a zombie and eating everybody's brainz tomorrow. All that's true?"

"Sure," Izzy said, quickly.

"*Izzy.*"

"You need to save the other kids, Dash." Her voice was super serious now. "You need to save them from Underhill. You need to save them from those brain-sucking headsets. That's all that matters."

The way she said it, there was no doubt she was telling the truth. Or I guess *I* was finally being honest with myself.

"Okay," I said. "So we'll write a book."

Izzy spun a circle in the air, like Jawz had just done in his fishbowl.

"But there's just one problem," I said.

Izzy stopped spinning.

"The power's out. That means no computer. No lights. How am I supposed to write a book without electricity?"

"We're gonna have to go *old school.*" Izzy grinned. Her teeth glowed white as she floated across my bedroom and drifted straight through the door.

"Old school?" I whispered aloud to my empty room.

"Yeah, dork," Izzy said, popping her head back through the door. Literally. *Through-the-door.* "Follow me, and I'll show you."

chapter 37

I TIPTOED behind Izzy as she floated through the house. I could hear my parents' voices murmuring from under their bedroom door. "*Dash*" this. "*Dash*" that. I'm sure they were worried about me. *I* was worried about me! I was following my imaginary friend through a dark house on a stormy night, planning to write a book.

What could go wrong?

Right?

I still didn't know what Izzy's plan was, or where she was leading me, or how I was actually going to write a book without a computer...

Come to think of it—there was a *bunch* of stuff that could go horribly wrong.

Izzy glared back over her ghost shoulder and put a pale blue finger to her lips.

I rolled my eyes. I forgot she could read my mind.

And then Izzy turned down the hall and disappeared into the second door on the right. Dad's office.

Izzy floated over to the printer and swiped a whole stack of paper. That made sense. But then she drifted through the closet door, and I couldn't—for the life of me —figure out why she was rummaging around in there.

I opened the door, trying to keep quiet, and that's when I saw it.

Dad's clunky old typewriter.

It was red with white keys and a chrome handle thingy. It kinda looked like the Ecto-1, the souped-up ambulance the Ghostbusters drove in the movie.

"Grab it," Izzy hissed. "That thing's way too heavy for a ghost to carry."

She was right. The typewriter weighed more than my backpack with every book stuffed in it (that is, when I went to a school that *had* books).

Izzy darted out of the closet and back down the hall. I fought to keep up, but the clunky typewriter was slowing me down. Coming out of the hall now, I could just see Izzy's pale blue glow drifting back up the stairs. I rounded the corner, put my foot on the first step, and dropped the typewriter.

Ka-*boom!*

The crash echoed up the stairs and down the hall.

I was just standing there, staring down at the freak-ishly heavy typewriter, when I heard the door at the end of the hall creak open. The master bedroom. *Mom and Dad's* room.

"Dash!" I looked up the steps, but Izzy wasn't there. "I'm in your head, dork. Grab the typewriter. Let's go!"

Footsteps came from down the hall, slow and sliding, feeling their way through the dark.

"Who–who's there?" I could tell it was Mom by her voice. She sounded scared. "Dash? Is that you?"

I realized she couldn't see me. The typewriter was turned upside down just below the bottom step. I squatted down and had it in my arms. Then I let go and stood.

"It's me, Mom," I whispered. "Dash."

"Oh. Thank goodness. Everything was so dark. I didn't know..."

Her voice trailed off, and I could definitely tell Mom was scared now. It made me wonder why Dad hadn't come? Why had he sent Mom out? I mean, it was just me, but what if it hadn't been? Then I remembered tomorrow was Halloween—the biggest day of the year for Kandy Brainz. Dad probably needed his rest.

"Yeah, Mom," I said, stepping between her and the typewriter, hoping she hadn't seen it. "It's just me."

"I've been so worried about you, Dash."

"I know."

"I just want you to be okay. You know? Sometimes I feel guilty for us having to move all the time. It's just that Kandy Brainz—"

"I know, Mom." I remembered how she said Dad was having a really tough time making sales this year. "But listen, everything's fine."

"You're sure?"

Her voice sounded scared, nothing like my Mystery-Machine-driving, Jimi-Hendrix-loving momma. And, heck no, I wasn't *sure*. Right now my only hope was to write a book. Like *that* was really gonna save the day.

"Yeah," I said and reached out, finding Mom's hand in the dark. Her fingers were cold against my palm. I squeezed them. "I'm sure."

We just stood there together for a moment, and then her hand was gone.

"I love you, Dash. Now try and get some sleep," Mom said. "I really want you to do well on that test tomorrow."

I waited until her feet started shuffling back down

the hall, and then I whispered, "I love you, too."

There was no light when Mom opened her bedroom door, just a low creaking sound, followed by a soft *thump* when it shut.

"What was all that about?" Izzy's words spanked against my eardrums. "There's no way you're getting *any* sleep tonight."

I stared down the hall a moment longer. I had the urge to burst into my parents' room, curl up in their bed, and just sleep forever, like Saturday mornings back when I was a little kid.

Instead, I turned and looked up the stairs. There was work to be done. Who knows, maybe Mom would be proud of me for writing a book.

The first step creaked under my foot, and then the second.

"Hey, dork?"

"Cut it with all the 'dork' stuff, Izzy."

"Okay, dummy. You're forgetting what we came down here for in the first place."

The typewriter's white keys grinned up at me from beneath the bottom step. I groaned, imagining having to lug it all the way up the stairs and into my room.

"What are you waiting for? We've got work to do." Izzy's voice tickled my brain. "Grab that thing and hurry up. Time is ticking!"

chapter 38

WRITING WITH A TYPEWRITER WAS WEIRD.

I had to figure out how to roll the paper into the machine. It took me forever to get the words lined up straight. The actual typing was hard, too. The keys were sticky, but when I got to the end of a line, a bell chimed. *Ding.* I liked that. I liked taking hold of the chrome handle thingy and sliding it back before I started the next sentence. I liked the sound the hammers made against the paper.

Thwack. Thwack.

There was just one problem: I didn't know what to write.

"Dash..." Izzy moaned, floating out of my nose again like a super-huge snot bubble. "You're not *writing* anything. You're just typing: 'My name is Dashiell Storey, but everybody calls me *Dash*.' Look. You've almost filled up a whole page with that one stinkin' line."

I pulled the paper out. That made a cool sound, too: *Raaappp.*

Looking down, I realized Izzy was right. I'd written the same sentence, again and again.

"What did you expect?" I snapped, wadding the paper into a ball. "I've never written a real book before. I have no idea what to write!" I chunked the paper into the trashcan beside my desk.

Izzy hovered above the typewriter. "Think about all the books you've read," she said. "Try to remember what you liked about them. That might help."

My brain spun as I tried to recall my favorite books. The creepy-cool covers. The first chapters. The first sentences. Then I realized they all had one thing in common.

"They start fast," I said.

"Fast?"

"Yeah, you know. They start with a *bang*. That's

what we need. Something that will make kids want to drop what they're doing and read."

"Hmmm." Izzy floated away from the desk, back across the room, and landed on my bed. "This might be tougher than I thought."

"And it doesn't help that these kids are already *addicted* to DarkNite," I said. "I bet some of them even skip meals just to try and level up. I wonder if any kid has ever like died from starvation because of video games?"

"That's it!" Izzy shot up off the bed in a blur. She was hovering over my desk again before I could blink. "Write that, Dash. Hurry! Go! Type what you just said."

"How the kids are addicted to DarkNite?"

Izzy nodded.

"Or the part about kids dying because of video games?"

"Yeah," Izzy yipped. "That part too. All of it. I think you really have something now."

Thwack. A hammer hit the paper.

Thwack. Thwack. Now there was a word.

And then it was like I wasn't in control anymore. My fingers pounded the keys as the hammers found their rhythm.

Sentences. Paragraphs. *Ding!*

A whole glorious page. *Raaappp!*

Rain pattered against the windows, lightning struck nearby and low thunder booms growled. I didn't notice. I was so lost in the words. It was like having the headset on again. Except, I was creating my own world this time, line by line.

The only light in the room came from Izzy. A pale blue glow. I had to squint to read the words as they flew from my fingers, but it was enough. Every once in a while, I'd pause to gather my thoughts. The room would go dark as Izzy drifted back inside my head.

"You good?" she'd whisper.

I didn't even have to say anything. I'd just think: *Yes.*

And then Izzy would say something goofy, like, "Cool beans," and slide out of my nose again.

The pages always looked different cast in Izzy's blue glow. My thoughtful pauses and Izzy's trips inside my head were our secret sauce. They kept things moving. Every time she re-emerged, I'd get new ideas. The plot would turn around in a way I wasn't expecting. I even doodled little pictures in the pages. They actually looked good! I'd never been able to draw like that before in my life, not without Izzy.

We carried on like this throughout the stormy night.

I lost track of time. My fingers flew faster and faster. There were more doodles. Pictures for every chapter!

My brain churned like a well-oiled machine. And then—all at once—it was over.

The only sound left in the room was the rain splattering against the window.

"Are you," Izzy whispered, "done?"

"I–I think so."

She zipped down to the pile of papers stacked on my desk and scooped them up.

"It's like heavy and everything," she said. "It actually *feels* like a book."

I didn't speak. I couldn't. All the words inside my head were out now, stamped forever on to those white sheets of paper.

Izzy darted down to the trashcan beside the desk and plucked out a plastic sack.

"What are you doing?"

Izzy said, "It's still raining," like that explained everything.

"So?"

"*So*, you don't want to get the pages all wet. Do you?"

I glanced up at the clock. It was just past three in the morning. I started for my bed, hoping the storm would be over when it was time to go to school.

"What are you doing?" she snapped.

"I just wrote a book, Izzy. I'm exhausted."

"Not yet you're not."

I was almost to my bed when what covers and pillows were left shot across the room and hit the wall. I fell face first on to my mattress anyway. I didn't need the sheets, or the pillows. I needed sleep.

"Dash!" Izzy yipped. "You're forgetting the most important part."

I rolled over as Izzy dropped the book in my lap. The plastic bag crinkled.

"Huh?"

"You've got to actually get somebody to *read* it. Like, before school starts. That way they can help spread the word."

I groaned. "What kid is going to be up this late at night? Or wait, I guess it's already morning."

Izzy grinned and floated toward the window. The rain slapped hard against the glass.

"Come on, dork. I'll show you."

chapter 39

As soon as I stepped out of my window and onto the roof, I wasn't tired anymore. Not with the wind whipping against my face, the rain coming down hard, and the thunder crackling in the distance.

Nope. No more Mr. Sleepy Head!

Izzy had it easy. She floated down to the front yard and was just hovering there now, waiting for me.

I took hold of the wet drainpipe and slid my way down.

That went better than expected.

"Hurry up, dork!" Izzy's voice blared inside my bleary head. "We don't have much time."

"Can't you warn me or something before you do that?"

"I'm serious, Dash. We have to get over to Colt's house and hope he's not already asleep."

"Colt?" I snapped. "Colt *Taylor?*"

"He's the coolest kid in sixth grade. I've told you this already. If he reads it and likes it—then everyone else will too."

"But, Izzy, it's three in the morning."

"I know. I *know.* That's why we have to hurry!"

I took a step forward, but I didn't mean to.

And then another.

Before I knew it—I was running.

"*Izzy,* cut it out! Are you like controlling my body, too?"

"We're the same person, Dash. I'm not controlling anything. Deep down you know Colt is our only hope. *That's* why you're running."

I tried not to think about it too hard. I was getting tired again, and wet. The rain was coming down harder now, smacking me in the face. I tucked the book under my shirt as my eyes scanned the dark neighborhood.

All the houses were pitch black. Not a light on anywhere.

"Duh," Izzy snorted, reading my mind again. "The power is still off."

"I'm not even sure where Colt lives, Izzy. I don't know where I'm going."

"Sure you do. Just look for the light."

There was a cul-de-sac up ahead of me. A house sat back in the far corner. A light glowed from the side window. A blue, flickering light.

"W-wait…" I stammered. "I thought the power was off?"

"Got me there," Izzy replied. "But that's Colt's house, and I'm guessing that's his window. The one with the blue light."

I made it under the edge of the Taylors' house and shook off the rain. I was so cold my teeth were chattering.

"I'm just supposed to tap on the window or something?"

Izzy appeared beside me and shook her head. "No, Dash. It's not that simple." She drifted over to the window, peered in, and then turned back to me. "You've got to convince Colt Taylor to read the book. You've got to sell it to him."

"Sell" was one of my least favorite words. I'd heard it too much over the years. Every time we had to move it was because Dad needed to *sell* more Kandy Brainz. Ugh. I really hated that word.

"Listen, Izzy." The night had turned so cold my breath came out in little wispy clouds. "I wrote the book, just like you told me to, but I never agreed to *sell* anything."

As I waited for Izzy to respond with some smart-alecky comment, I leaned over and peeked in Colt Taylor's window. He was just sitting there with a controller in his hand. The flickering blue light came from a gigantic television screen. I think it was even bigger than mine. *Wait.* The whole neighborhood's power was still down. Where was Colt getting electricity?

I expected Izzy to read my mind again, call me a "dork," and offer a logical explanation. So I just kept standing there, staring in the window, waiting...

"Izzy?"

I turned. She was far away from me now, almost back out in the road, but I could hear her voice clearly.

"I can't help you with this one, Dash. It's for your own good."

"What! No!" I shouted, not even thinking about how I was still standing so close to Colt's window.

"Yes, Dash," Izzy said. "You've got to do this part alone."

I could see her blue glow fading. I called out for her again, but then she was gone.

A loud *creak* echoed out through the night and crawled up my spine. I turned back, slowly, toward the window.

"Dash?" Colt grunted with a look on his face like he'd just seen a ghost. "It's three in the morning—*and* it's raining. What are you doing out here?"

Good question.

chapter 40

"W HEN FACED WITH A STICKY QUESTION, *Dash-man,
always return fire with another, stickier question.*" That
was one of Dad's candy-selling commandments. I could
hear his voice in my head now instead of Izzy's. Things
were getting weirder by the second.

"Uh..." I mumbled. "Were you playing a video
game? How do you still have power?"

I could tell by the look on Colt's face, he wasn't
buying it.

"I'm still mad at you, man."

"What'd I do?"

"Almost three months at Haven Middle School,"

Colt said, "and I never, not once, got sent to the Principal's office. Not until you came along."

"*I* was the one that got suspended," I snapped. "I took the fall for you. Why do you think Principal Manson just sent you back to class?"

Colt's forehead wrinkled.

"I told Manson I jacked your headset. I told her *I* was the one playing DarkNite."

"You're serious? I thought I was just cool enough to not get in trouble."

When he said that, I really wanted to turn and walk away. Surely there was some other kid who could read the book. But, honestly, I was too curious about that glow coming from his room.

"You never answered my question," I said. "How are you getting electricity?"

Colt nodded back to his monstrous TV and grinned. "Cool, huh?"

"Yeah, sure, but I thought the power was out?"

Colt's smile widened. "You ever heard of a generator?"

"Yes," I lied. "Of course I have."

"It's like a gas-powered engine-thingy that makes electricity when the power goes down."

The book felt small and pointless in my arms. Colt

was further gone than I thought. The kid had a *generator* in his room so he could play video games.

"It's not mine," Colt said, quickly. "My dad is super obsessed with doomsday prepping."

"Doomsday what?"

"Dad's got a whole closet full of water jugs, toilet paper, and Cheetos. He says Cheetos never go bad. *Never.*"

"I–I—" The words rattled out through my chattering teeth. "I don't have a clue what you're talking about."

"My dad's a doomsday prepper. You know... He's trying to get prepared for the end of the world. The zombie apocalypse, or whatever."

I bit down on my bottom lip hard enough to keep my teeth from clacking together. It was time to get serious. Izzy's words came back into my head: *You've got to sell it to him.*

"So, your dad believes in zombies?" I asked.

Colt shrugged. "It's raining really hard, Dash. What are you doing out here?"

I took a deep breath. "I have something I want to give you."

"Why didn't you say so?" Colt leaned out over the window and offered me his hand. "Here, let me help you inside."

I stepped back and took the bag from under my arm. The plastic crinkled as I slid the book out. It was a little damp, but I could still read the title on the front page. I realized I'd forgotten one of the most important parts—the cover! It didn't matter. The look on Colt's face, it was obvious he wasn't buying it.

"Ah, gross!" Colt snarled, pointing. "Is that a *book?*"

He jumped back like I was holding a rattlesnake and took hold of the window. Another loud creak cut through the night as Colt started to slam it shut. Without even thinking, I slid the book over the sill just as the window came down.

Clomp.

Luckily, the book was right side up. Colt stared down at the title and squinted his eyes.

"This book," he said and lifted the window just high enough to pull the stack of paper into his room, "it's about *zombies?*"

"Kinda."

Colt thumbed through the pages. "It's got your name on the front."

"I wrote it."

The window slid up and didn't make as much noise this time.

"You wrote this whole thing?" Colt gasped, dangling his head out the window again. "Why?"

"Because..." I said, but then the rain stopped all at once, like someone had turned off a giant faucet. The whole neighborhood went eerily quiet. "I, uh, I wrote it because I thought it might help."

Colt ran his fingers across the front page. "It does have a cool title, but where's the cover?"

"I just wrote it tonight. I was in a hurry. I guess I forgot about the cover..."

Colt glanced back over his shoulder at the glowing television screen. "And you want me to read this whole thing? Like *tonight?*"

"Before school."

"Well..." Colt said. "Dad's generator only has so much juice. So I guess if it goes out, I might could give your book a try."

He paused and I held my breath

"But I was just about to level up in DarkNite," Colt said. "There's not a single kid in all of Haven Middle School that's a Level 83. Not even any of the eighth graders. And I always level up faster when I play on my flat screen. I can see so much more. It's like..."

I let out a long rush of air, but Colt just kept talking. I knew there was no chance he was going to read my book. Not tonight. Not with that glowing screen calling his name and only a few more hours before the first bell rang.

I turned without saying anything and started to walk away.

"Hey, wait. I just read the first line," Colt whispered across the quiet night. "It says this book could save my life?"

I stopped but didn't turn back to him. I didn't want to come off as desperate. That was another one of Dad's candy-selling commandments: *"You can't want it more than they do."*

"Save my life, huh?" Colt said. "That's kinda freaky."

"What if I told you a ghost helped me write it?"

"I wouldn't believe you."

"Says the kid whose Dad has a bunker stocked and ready for the zombie apocalypse."

I didn't say anything for a few seconds, letting my epic burn sizzle.

Then Colt said, "So there's zombies in it, too?"

"Read the book, Colt. See for yourself," I said and started walking away again, really thinking I'd sealed the deal. I got all the way out to the road before I looked back.

It started with a flicker, and then there was a burst of light, windows around the neighborhood buzzing and thrumming again with electricity.

The power was back on.

Through the open window, I watched Colt Taylor plop down on the floor and take hold of the controller. My book was just sitting on the foot of his bed, and I knew—right then—Colt would never read it.

FRIDAY

chapter 41

THREE SHARP KNOCKS at my window were the first things I heard Friday morning.

Tap. Tap. Tap.

I rolled over and remembered it was Halloween, the day of the Z.O.M. Test. I blinked against the sunlight creeping in through the bedroom window. My crusty eyes fought hard to focus. Fragmented memories from the night before floated to the surface of my brain and drifted away: the storm, writing the book, Colt Taylor and Izzy Hendrix.

Three more knocks on the window. Louder than before.

I had a guess who it was, and honestly, I didn't want to talk to her.

"Go away, Izzy."

Tap. Tap. Tap.

"Colt didn't read the book," I grumbled. "Okay? It's over."

Tap. Tap. Tap.

I felt around in bed for a pillow. I wanted to throw it at the window. Maybe that would shut Izzy up, but my pillow was gone.

I sat up and saw all my bedding in a pile beside my desk. Then I remembered how Izzy had flown them around the room the night before.

My feet hit the ground and I started for the window, ready to scream at Izzy until the veins in my neck turned purple and I saw little twinkling stars. I couldn't see anything out the window because the sun was just coming up and shining right in my eyes. I threw the window open, and that's when I heard:

"Who's Izzy?"

Colt Taylor sat perched on my rooftop, holding a thick stack of wrinkled, white paper in his hands.

"That's my book. You–you actually read my book?"

"Wait," Colt said, eyes getting wider. "*Izzy!* The girl

from your book! She's real?" He clapped his hands together like a baby. "Dash! You *have* to let me meet her!"

I stood there, still fully dressed from the night before. "You really read the book?"

"Every single page," Colt said, scooting up closer to the window. "And it was completely redonk. I loved it!"

Warm fuzzies floated up from my stomach and into my head.

"I loved it so much," Colt said, reaching behind his back, "I made *this!*"

It was a piece of thick paper with five black words stamped across the front. It took me a moment to realize what it was, and then it hit me.

"You made a *cover* for my book?"

Colt flashed a toothy grin. "You likey?"

I was shocked. My mouth froze up. I couldn't think of what to say.

Colt took the paper in both hands, like he was going to wad it up.

But before he did, I shouted, "Wait! *Colt.* That's the nicest thing anybody's ever done for me. I love it."

He rolled his eyes. "Don't get all gushy on me. We still got work to do."

The sun inched its way up over the vacant, creepy-looking house on the corner of Coventry Drive. The one where I used to think Izzy Hendrix lived.

"Work?" I said. "What do you mean?"

"Just like in your book. We've got to save the sixth-graders and make sure Underhill doesn't eat our brainz!"

Colt caught his breath and just kept staring at me.

"I mean, wait," he whispered. "Your book *is* true, isn't it?"

Where was Izzy when I needed her? I tried thinking her name really hard.

Izzzzzzy.

Nothing.

No blue glow. No snarky comments.

For once in my life, I really wanted to be called a dork.

But there was only silence, brain crickets chirping inside my head. And Colt was still sitting there on my roof, waiting for me to tell him the truth about Mr. Underhill, the truth about zombies.

"Uh," I stammered, trying to think of what Izzy would say. "You believed it, right?"

"I stayed up all night reading it. I drew you an awesome cover. So, yeah... I believed every word."

"Why?"

Colt put a finger to his mouth and looked up. "I

dunno. The power came back on, and I was ready to level up in DarkNite, but then I read the first page."

He paused and looked straight at me.

"Then I read the next page, and the one after that, and then I couldn't stop."

"Why?"

"Quit asking me that."

"I mean, why did you like it so much?"

"Oh," Colt said. "That's easy. I liked it because it all sounded so real. I mean, Underhill is a freak-a-zoid and the whole class is beyond addicted to the headsets. So, yeah, it all just made sense."

I lifted one blue Chuck onto the windowsill and wished hard for Izzy to appear. She'd helped so much with the book. I wanted her to hear how much Colt liked it. But she was gone, and for some reason, I worried I might never see her again.

"You're climbing out the window?" Colt raised both eyebrows and stared at my shoes.

"Like you said, we've got work to do."

"Couldn't I just climb in and then we could walk out the front door?"

"You read the book, right?"

Colt scrunched his nose and pointed to his creepy-cool cover as proof.

"Think about it," I said, all the way out on the roof

now. "Don't you remember the part where Dash and Colt slide down the drainpipe and run all the way to school before the teachers get there?"

"Was that in there?" Colt yipped. "I can't remember. I read it really fast."

I'd already slid my way down the roof and was close to the gutter now. I took hold of the drainpipe with both hands. "If it wasn't in the book before," I shouted. "It's about to be!"

chapter 42

As we ran across Haven, taking the well-worn path past Coventry Pond, through downtown where I counted one—just *one!*—pumpkin painted on the Walmart's glass window, I tried to get things straight in my head.

Izzy was my imaginary friend. She was a part of me. She lived inside of me. But for some reason, she had disappeared.

And the book I wrote—the one Colt Taylor read and loved so much he created that amazing cover—it was true.

Right?

Okay, at least it was *mostly* true. I basically just told the story like it happened. I mean, I did have a crazy imagination, and sometimes I got confused about reality (I'm sure you know this by now) but surely I wouldn't have lied about something as serious as zombies.

The only thing I couldn't really remember writing was the end.

Maybe I was still writing it...

Weird.

By the time Colt and I made it to Haven Middle School, the sun was up over the tree line, painting the sky in cotton-candy swirls. I wasn't sure what time it was, but there wasn't a single car in the parking lot.

"How-do-we," Colt heaved, trying to catch his breath, "get-in... the-school?"

I wanted to ask Izzy what to do next, but then it came to me.

"The window," I rasped. "Underhill's window. He leaves it unlocked because, well, he's a lazy brain muncher."

"Yeah!" Colt shouted. "Let's go."

He disappeared around the corner of the school. Colt was freaky fast. Maybe even faster than Izzy. By the time I caught up with him, he was dangling from Mr. Underhill's window, legs kicking and squirming behind him.

"You were right!" he squawked. "It was open and everything, just like in the book."

"Uh, yeah," I mumbled and followed Colt in through the window.

The school was all quiet and eerie without any teachers or kids. It felt familiar, like when I had played DarkNite and Izzy led me down the hall.

"The teachers' lounge," Colt said, pointing. "That's where they keep the copier."

And then he was gone again, already sprinting through the floppy lounge door.

I waited a second before following him. I wanted to make sure there was no one else in the hall. The school was so quiet I could hear myself breathing. All clear.

When I finally made it to the lounge door, I peeked inside. Everything was going perfectly to plan. Colt had the copier running like an old pro (he *was* a teacher's pet, I'm sure he'd been sent to the teachers' lounge a bazillion times to make copies). Mounds of paper filled the printer's tray. Each stack even had Colt's freaky cover stapled to the front.

We were making *books!*

I was so excited, I almost didn't hear the footsteps coming down the hall.

Slow, sliding, *creeping* steps.

I turned just in time to see Underhill zombie-walking his way straight for me. He looked worse than ever. His wormy hair swished and swayed like a den of dancing snakes. His yellow teeth. His black doll eyes.

Closer and closer.

But I couldn't move. I was frozen with fear.

He was only ten feet away from the teachers' lounge now.

So close I could smell his barf breath.

Underhill opened his mouth, really wide, like he was ready for a Dash-brain appetizer, but then he just sneezed.

Ahhh-chooo!

I was still standing there, still frozen, watching Underhill wipe his nose with the back of his shirtsleeve, when a strong hand jerked me so hard from behind I fell backwards through the teachers' lounge door.

chapter 43

I CRASHED hard into the huge pile of already stacked books. Papers flew up and fluttered like maple seed pods, helicoptering their way down to the linoleum floor.

"You good?"

I turned and saw Colt with papers on his head and shoulders. Papers everywhere. I realized he was the one who had jerked me out of the hall.

"Yeah," I said. "You saved me."

"Not yet." Colt stood up quick and was back at the

door before I could blink. "Whatever happens, Dash, you make sure the other kids read this book."

He put his hand on the door like he was ready to leave.

"Wait!" I cried. "Underhill's still out there. I'm sure he saw me. I'm sure he heard—"

"I know," Colt said. "But listen, you saved my butt once, and now you're about to save our entire class. I think it's time I finally returned the favor."

Before Colt could open the door, it started to open on its own. Slowly. Inch by inch.

"It's *Underhill!*" I screeched.

Colt threw his shoulder into the door and pushed it shut, at least for the moment.

"I'll distract him. I'll tell him I was trying to study or something. He'll believe me, Dash, but listen..." Colt pushed harder on the door and gritted his teeth. "You've got to get those books printed off. You've got to get them in every kids' desk before it's time to start the test."

"But how will they even know the books are in there?"

Colt flashed his million-dollar smile. "Leave that part to me. I can spread the word on the DarkNite message board before we get started." He paused and his smile dissolved into his game face. "But you've got to get these books in there, Dash. Can I count on you?"

"I–I'll do it," I said. "I promise."

Colt leaned back and gave me his patented, corny thumbs up. Except, this time it didn't look so corny.

And then the door flung open. Colt was so quick, though—so freaky fast—he slipped out through the crack before Underhill had a chance to look inside.

I could hear their voices murmuring from the other side. Colt did just like he said. He went right into his brown-nosing routine, telling Underhill how he'd gotten to school early so he could study.

Then I heard a strange beeping sound coming from behind me. I turned. What I saw kinda looked like a car wreck. Like a pileup on the interstate.

The printer had jammed.

Red lights flashed and blinked. The beeping sound seemed to get louder and louder.

I checked the clock. There were just a few minutes left before the first bell would ring and the other kids would come pouring in from the playground. And *then* it'd be time for the Z.O.M Test.

I slapped machine, hard. It didn't help. All those years spent reading creepy books and watching scary movies didn't help at all when it came to fixing copiers.

"Izzy," I whispered. "Izzy, please. I need your help."

The only sound in the teachers' lounge was the copier, beeping angrily again and again.

Then I heard something. A voice softer than a whisper.

"*I–I—*"

I put my hands over my ears. The voice was coming from inside my head.

"*I'm here, Dash. I'm always here.*"

"Izzy!" I cried. "Izzy, please. Just listen. I don't know how to fix the copier, and if I don't fix it then—"

It was like I could hear her fading away. A faint whir, and then nothing.

I took a deep breath and went straight for the buzzing copier.

Okay, so slapping the thing didn't work. Maybe there was like an instruction manual or something. I scanned the floor. There were papers everywhere. Papers from my book mixed in with teachers' papers. Tests and worksheets everywhere.

My brain spun as I bent down, pawing at the mess. That's just what I was doing when the beeping finally stopped.

I looked up, and I swear, the copier was covered in a soft blue glow.

"Izzy?"

A paper shot out and landed in the printer's tray. Then more papers, falling neatly into perfect stacks.

Soon the machine was chugging along again,

pumping out book after book, even stapling Colt's awesome cover to the front.

"*Izzy!*" I shouted, collecting the rest of the papers from the floor. "You did it!"

I waited as the last of the books finished copying, dying to hear Izzy's voice again. I checked the clock. There were only two minutes left before the first bell rang. The books were done printing now, but I just kept waiting.

I whispered Izzy's name one more time as I took the heavy stack of books from the printer's tray. I was almost out the door, when I finally heard what I was waiting for.

"*You* did it, dork."

I'm not gonna lie. I was so happy I almost cried.

"Okay, *okay*," I said and wiped my eyes. "I did it."

I stepped out into the hall, carrying that ginormous stack of papers, and then the bell rang.

chapter 44

As THE STUDENTS flooded in from early morning recess, I made a mad dash for Mr. Underhill's classroom.

The door was unlocked, which I thought was weird, but honestly, I didn't have time to think about it too hard. I went right to work shoving books into the desks, and that's when I heard Mr. Underhill's voice.

"...but, Colt, I still don't understand why my classroom window was wide open?"

I turned. Mr. Underhill had his back to me, talking to Colt over by the open window. Colt winked in my direction and then gave Mr. Underhill his game-winning grin.

"I dunno, Mr. U..." Colt pleaded. "Maybe it's like a mystery or something?"

I realized Colt was distracting Underhill so I could get all the books in the desk, and then a strange thought flashed through my mind: Was Colt Taylor like my new best friend?

I went from desk to desk, stuffing each book into the shallow tray underneath.

Book after book.

Desk after desk.

I shoved the last book in the last desk just as the rest of the kids filed in through the door.

"Ah," Mr. Underhill exclaimed, turning away from Colt. "Welcome, students. It's the day we've all been waiting for!"

As I took my seat in the back row, I finally got a good look at Mr. Underhill. His skin was paler than usual. There were strands of his greasy hair stuck to his forehead, like he was sweating. Everything about him seemed frail, almost sickly. Everything except his eyes.

"It's finally here!" Mr. Underhill wheezed, his hungry eyes dancing across the domes of the other students. "The Zone One Marker Test!" Spit flew from his lips as he talked, like his mouth was watering. "Class will run a little differently during testing today."

Colt weaved his way across the classroom and sat down in his desk as Underhill continued his speech.

"Once the test is underway, your headsets will enter 'Lockdown Mode.'" Underhill bared his yellow teeth, grinning. "So that means you won't be able to access any other browsers, especially not DarkNite."

The blood drained from my face. Colt was supposed to send word to the class on the DarkNite message board. That's how they were going to know to look in their desks for the book.

I watched Colt's shoulders go stiff. We didn't have a chance now.

And then Izzy's words rattled through my mind. I didn't actually hear her talking this time. I just remembered last night, when the power was out and I couldn't imagine how I'd write a book without a computer, Izzy had said: *We're gonna have to go old school.*

That was it!

I dug around in my desk for some paper and a pencil. Luckily, my fingers rolled over a pencil, but I couldn't find a single sheet of paper.

"Okay, class," Mr. Underhill droned. "Those of you who aren't already wearing your headsets, it's time to strap 'em on!"

My fingers slapped the metal tray, but there wasn't any paper in the desk. Most all the other students had their headsets on now. Colt glanced at me over his shoulder.

"What are we going to do?" he whispered.

I closed my eyes just as my fingers found something in the desk tray.

The *book!*

Colt was still looking at me as I ripped the last page off the book, trying to be as quiet as possible. "We're about to go *old school*," I whispered, keeping the paper in my lap, scribbling a note to the rest of my classmates. I couldn't help but think maybe I was writing the real end of the book right then. *Weird.*

The note was simple. It read:

 Fellow Classmates,

> *There's a zombie book in your desk. Read it instead of taking Underhill's stupid test. Pass the note along until everybody sees it.*
> *Sincerely...*

I pushed the note up and over Colt's shoulder.

His forehead scrunched as he scanned the words, and then his eyes lit up.

"Oh, I get it—*old* school."

"Yup," I whispered. "Now you just need to sign it."

"What? Why me?"

I leaned up, keeping my eyes on Underhill fidgeting with another student's headset in the front row. "You're the coolest kid in sixth grade, Colt. If that note is from you, then they will actually read it."

Colt flashed his pearly whites and scribbled his name on the paper. "You really think I'm the coolest kid in school?"

"I said *sixth grade*. Don't be ridiculous."

Colt was still grinning as he passed the note to the girl sitting in front of him. She read it and quickly passed it along. The boy sitting in front of her did the same, and on and on it went.

It was kinda cool to see the Haven kids going *old school*. I bet they'd never passed a note in class before. They were surprisingly good at it.

Every time Mr. Underhill would turn his back to help adjust a headset, the note would pass. Slipping from hand to hand. Silently. It was like a game, and my classmates were definitely having fun.

I watched their faces as they read the note. Watched their hands as they slapped around in the desks and found the surprise I'd left them.

Just as the note finally made it back to my desk, Mr. Underhill cleared his throat and said, "All right, class. Your headsets will now be entering 'Lockdown Mode.'"

The timing was perfect. All the students looked just

like they were supposed to—like they were actually taking the Z.O.M. Test. Sitting there, very quiet and very still, with their headsets on, but all of their eyes were looking down. If I listened close, I could hear the pages turning in their laps.

Mr. Underhill hobbled back toward the front of the class. He strapped his headset on and propped his feet up on his desk. I knew he wouldn't move again, not until the test was over.

It was a funny feeling, sitting there, knowing all the kids were reading my book. Would they like it? Would they *hate* it? Would it actually hold their attention long enough to keep them from taking the Z.O.M. Test?

Stop asking so many questions, dork.

Izzy?

I waited.

Is that you?

Nothing.

I started chewing my bottom lip. Deep down, I feared I'd never see Izzy Hendrix again, but then I looked at the book in my lap. Colt's crazy-cool cover. The title I liked so much. It was Izzy's idea to spell "Brainz" with a "Z". She thought it would look cool. It did.

I flipped the book open and read the first line: "*This book could save your life. I'm serious, dead serious.*"

I remembered how Izzy had helped me come up with that line too. I kept reading. It didn't take long for Izzy's character to show up in the book. My first day at Haven Middle School. Izzy telling me to keep my eyes closed when the headset flickered to life. She was everywhere. She was a huge part of the story. Izzy Hendrix was on nearly every page. It was almost like she was back again.

I just kept reading, enjoying all the good times I'd had with Izzy. And I guess everybody else kept reading, too. By the time the bell rang and the test was over, half my class was crying, the other half was peeved, but they were *all* asking the same question:

"How does it end?"

the (REAL) end

IF YOU HAVEN'T GUESSED it by now, the book you've been reading is the same one that saved my class: *Books Make Brainz Taste Bad*. I always loved that title. Colt did too. That's why he stamped it across the cover in those big, bold letters.

The only thing that's different is the end. I didn't really know how to finish the book, at least not at first.

When I took it over for Colt to read that night, I just had to make something up. Honestly, I've been making stuff up all along, but the message is the important part—books really can save your life.

This book saved me. It saved the other sixth graders, too. They read the whole thing in Mr. Underhill's class that day instead of taking the Z.O.M. Test.

That's right.

Nobody took the test.

And Mr. Underhill's lazy butt was too busy vegging out on his headset to notice.

By the time the test was over, right about the time all the kids finished reading my book and started asking me questions about the end—Principal Manson barged into our classroom.

Underhill never saw her coming. He still had his feet propped up and his headset on. Principal Manson was super ticked. She slapped his combat boots off the desk, yanked his headset away from his eyes, and growled, "None of your students took the test! There wasn't a single question answered from this class!"

Underhill didn't say anything. Not even when Principal Manson took him by the ear and started dragging him out the door.

We never saw him again.

Now, wait, before your imagination goes all bonkers, let me tell you the truth this time: Underhill was not a zombie.

He was just a really bad teacher.

Maybe, deep down, I knew Underhill wasn't a zombie all along. But sometimes it's nice to make up stories. Sometimes zombies are easier to defeat than bad teachers, or distracted parents, or moving to a new town and not having any friends.

So, no, Principal Manson didn't lock Underhill up in some super-secret zombie prison.

She just fired him. That's why we never saw him again.

Or at least that's what Colt said. He'd heard his mom and dad talking before he came over to my house on Halloween night.

Yup...

Colt Taylor, the coolest sixth grader at Haven Middle School, came to *my* house on Halloween night. And he was even wearing a creeptastic zombie costume with one bloody eyeball dangling down off his chin.

Colt wasn't the only kid that made a stop at the Storey house that night.

My classmates passed the book along to their brothers and sisters when they got home from school. Third graders. Fourth graders. Even a few seventh and *eighth* graders—they all read *Brainz*, and by Friday night, everybody was ready to go trick-or-treating.

The streets of my neighborhood were filled with

zombies! Wait, I mean, kids *dressed* as zombies. It was perfect: a crisp fall night, the moon hanging just over the top of the creepy old house on the corner, glowing orange like a jack-o'-lantern. But there was just one problem...

None of the grownups had any candy.

Luckily, when all those parents realized their kids actually wanted to go trick-or-treating this year, Dad was ready.

Kandy Brainz to the Rescue!

Every kid in Haven got one of Dad's gigantic, sugar-filled brainz by the end of the night. They were so big, some of the smaller kids couldn't even carry them. Dad made more sales in Haven than he had in any town before.

For a few hours, the streets were crawling with monsters and ghosts, witches and zombies. There were a few hardcore DarkNite fans in all black suits. *The Man In Black Lives!* Dr. Blackwell even made an appearance. He stopped by the house just long enough to tell me he was proud that I'd finally told a *true* story. Whatever that means.

Eventually, the houses started running out of candy. Pretty soon the whole neighborhood was dark and Haven's first legit Halloween was officially over.

Colt and I made our way back over to my house.

When we got there, Mom and Dad were sitting out on the front porch steps, waiting for us.

"And who is this?" Dad said, still beaming from selling so much candy.

I turned and looked at Colt Taylor. The fake blood. The dangling eyeball. I almost told Dad he was just some zombie I'd found wandering around the neighborhood in search of juicy brainz. But before I could make my lame joke, Colt stepped forward.

"My name's Colt Taylor, and I'm—" He cut his eyes at me, his *real* eyes not the fake one hanging off his chin. "I'm Dash's new *best* friend."

The way Dad smiled, it was different. Even bigger than when all the parents had come around ready to buy his candy. It was the biggest smile I'd ever seen. Mom smiled too as she took hold of Dad's arm and put her head on his shoulder.

"Is that true, Dash-man?" Dad said, looking at me.

I hesitated, for just one second, and that's when I felt something sliding slowly out of my nose. I blinked as the world turned a pale shade of blue. When I opened my eyes, Izzy Hendrix was hovering right there in front of me.

She didn't say anything, and nobody else did either. I knew they couldn't see her.

Izzy floated down, coming straight for me. I thought

maybe she was going to zip inside my head again. Maybe she'd decided to stay a while longer.

I was wrong.

She kissed me on the cheek. Her lips were light and warm like hot cocoa steam. Before I could speak, before I could tell her she'd always be my *first* best friend, she floated up, higher and higher, blending in with the huge orange moon hanging over her creepy old house, and then she was gone.

"Uh, *Dash?*" Colt's voice shook me from Izzy's spell. "Don't leave me hanging."

"Yeah," I managed, looking down from the sky. "Colt is my friend."

"*Best* friend," Colt said, grinning up at Dad. "I'm sure you know this already, Mr. Storey, but Dash gets kinda shy sometimes."

Dad just stood there, smiling.

"Well, we have some news to share," Mom said, letting go of Dad's arm as she stood and made her way down the steps. "Your father just heard from his bosses at Kandy Brainz. They were so impressed with his record-setting sales tonight, they've asked if we'd be willing to stay in Haven for a little while longer." She paused, staring straight at me. "What do you think about that, Dash?"

"You mean, we wouldn't have to move next year?" I said and looked to the sky.

"That's right," Mom said, smiling. "Haven would be our new home."

I swear I could see a blue afro sprouting up and out in all directions around the moon. It gave me hope. Maybe Izzy would be back.

"What do you say, Dash-man?" Dad said. "Sound like a deal?"

I was so happy, I couldn't speak.

"Quit being weird." Colt elbowed me in the ribs and looked over at Mom and Dad. "Of course Dash is stoked about staying in Haven. *I'm* in Haven!"

"Yeah," I laughed, walking up the steps to hug my parents. "I guess that's right."

Mom had her arms out, welcoming me to our new home. I was almost there...

"You *guess?*" Colt snorted. "Dash... Wait until I tell you about the teacher Principal Manson hired to replace Underhill."

I turned around, slowly. Colt had this super serious look on his face.

"What's so weird about the new teacher?"

"Just wait," Colt said, grinning now. "After you meet this creeper, it'll be time to write the *next* book."

THE END!

(for now...)

Dash Storey is back
to face another creeper in . . .

BMBTB2
Witch Hunt!

TURN THE PAGE FOR A SPECIAL SNEAK PEEK!

UNDER PRESSURE

How much is a story worth? Like a really good one. Your all-time favorite movie. That tattered book you know by heart.

A real, *true* story is worth dying for.

Or at least I hope it is, because that's exactly what I'm doing right now—*dying*.

Drowning, to be exact. Sinking faster and faster. Like I'm being pulled down. And my life isn't flashing before my eyes, but instead every stupid choice I've made over the last week is pulsing on repeat through my brain, a highlight reel of Dash Storey's most epic fails.

I know this much—one dumb story isn't worth what I'm feeling right now.

But that's what started all this. A story. I just wanted to write the next *BMBTB* (*Books Make Brainz Taste Bad*) book. I *wanted* to, but I couldn't.

The farther I fall, the deeper down I go, the colder the water gets. And there's like this crazy pressure pushing against my eardrums.

Pressure.

I couldn't write the next book because of pressure. Not after *BMBTB* hit every best-seller list in the country, and then my publisher started mailing checks to my house with too many zeros to count. There was no way I could live up to all that hype.

It should've been easy. I know how to tell a story. There are only three parts: the beginning, the middle, and the grand finale! But I was drowning under the weight of that next book. I kept trying to write, but nothing came out. So I did the one thing I'd just told all the other kids in Haven *never* to do...

BMBTB2: WITCH HUNT
COMING SOON!
(whenever Dash gets around to writing it)

about the author

"Eli Cranor" is the pen name (fake name) of Dash Storey. When *Books Make Brainz Taste Bad* was first published, the marketing team thought the name "Dash" sounded too young.

Coincidently, there is a real man named Eli Cranor who lives in Arkansas with his wife and two kids. He's been known to make school visits and claim he's the real author of the book. If he shows up at your school, don't believe a word he says.

www.elicranor.com

acknowledgments

Thanks to Johnny Wink for loving words in a contagious kind of way. Ten years later, I'm still putting the black on the white, and it all started with you. Thanks to Mike Sutton for always having my back (not to mention the pro bono legal work, the late-night phone calls, and the Christmas gifts for my kids). Thanks to Alex Taylor for still being my friend even after I published this book.

Thanks Jack Butler for teaching me how to use my words. Thanks to Ace Atkins for always helping out. Thanks to William Boyle and Jimmy Cajoleas for showing kindness when I needed it most. Thanks to Jerry Spinelli for preparing me for when "the game begins." Thanks to Hannah West and Sarah Goodman for the guidance.

Thanks to the ARWDC: Josh Wilson, John Post, and Travis Simpson. We need to get together soon!

Thanks to my young readers: Brayden, Jack, Penelope, Mattie, Colton, and Chloe. Y'all were right, kids don't say "totes" anymore. And, Brayden, keep writing. One day we'll all be reading YOUR books!

Thanks to Nina Bolton for giving me a teacher's perspective. Thanks to Dr. T for being Dr. T. Thanks to Ariana "The Canadian Positivity Ninja" Townsend for reading this book while pregnant and offering such sage advice. Thanks to Pat Young for the early read and for running the best durn bookstore in the universe (Dog Ear Books)!

Thanks to Dustin Brady, R.L. Ullman, and Connor Grayson for showing me the way.

Thanks, especially, to Daniel Freeman for the amazing artwork and the never-say-die attitude you brought to this project.

Thanks to Mom for always being my biggest fan.

Thanks to Dad for always shooting me straight.

Thanks to Emmy for asking me, over and over again, to see this book (I hope you like it, sis).

Thanks to Fin (you're not even one year old yet, but you're my son, so...)

And most of all, thanks to Mal. You're my rock. The yin to my yang. Thank you, baby, for everything.

—Eli Cranor

about the illustrator

Daniel Freeman met Dash Storey in art class before he moved to Haven. Ever since that fateful summer day, Daniel's been secretly helping Dash perfect his creep-tastic drawing style. Daniel lives in Arkansas with his wife and daughter where he runs his own art studio called Kaleidoclasm.

www.kaleidoclasm.art

facebook.com/kaleidoclasm

twitter.com/kaleidoclasm

instagram.com/kaleidoclasm

Made in the USA
Columbia, SC
07 September 2020